RESURRECTION MARY

A GHOST STORY

RESURRECTION MARY

MARY

ೲ

A GHOST STORY
ೲ

BY
KENAN
HEISE

Published by
Chicago Historical Bookworks
Evanston, Illinois
1990

OTHER BOOKS BY
KENAN HEISE

They Speak for Themselves:
Interviews with the Destitute of Chicago

The Death of Christmas
(with Arthur Allan)

Is There Only One Chicago

How to Survive in Chicago and Enjoy It
(with Charles McWhinnie, Judith Birnbaum,
and Juanita Carlson)

The Journey of Silas B. Bigelow

Chicago Center for Enterprise
(with Michael Edgerton)

Aunt Ella Stories

Hands on Chicago
(with Mark Frazel)

Alphonse:
A Play about Al Capone in His Own Words

The Chicagoization of America: 1893-1917

Chicago Originals:
A Cast of the City's Colorful Characters
(with Ed Baumann)

831 Main St. Evanston, IL 60202

10 9 8 7 6 5 4 3 2 1

ISBN: 0-924772-09-3

Chicago Historical Bookworks
831 Main Street
Evanston, IL 60202

Printed in the U.S.A.

Illustration, cover, design, editing, typesetting
by Dorothy Kavka, Evanston, IL 60202

ಌ

To Susan Brady
and all other Southwest Siders

ಌ

છ

ACKNOWLEDGEMENTS
છ

Special thanks to
Dorothy and Becky Kavka, Ruth Buck, John Lux, Rose DeVito,
Susan Brady, and members of my family.

❦

Evil is and evil promises.

❦

PROLOGUE

The southwest suburbs of Chicago
---

5 P.M., Friday, September 6, 1968

"You wanta know what I'm gonna take tonight, Junior?"

"You gonna steal something else from old Sarge. His wallet, maybe?"

"No, dummy, I'm gonna take her."

"What? Who's her?"

"Janice."

"You gonna get a piece, Eddie?"

"Naw. I am going to get all of it."

The two young men sat, as they usually did after work, on the bank of the Sanitary and Ship Canal just north of the Southwest Expressway leading out of Chicago. Junior was disappointed. He would rather talk about what Eddie had stolen that day.

The city room of a newspaper office on Michigan Avenue in Chicago
---

Jim held in his hand the ticket stub he had found while cleaning out Paul's desk. The memories that came with the memento focused his eyes as though he were looking back through time.

Once again, it was nine years earlier, October 1, 1959

The home-run ball off the bat of White Sox first baseman Ted Kluszewski arched only slightly as it shot toward the bunting-decked stands of Comiskey Park. Paul Kowalski bounced up out of his seat, clapping his hands, his body swaying with the abandon of an old-time religionist at a Southern Baptist revival.

"Christ," Jim Rooney said with a gasp. Slowly, he rose next to Paul, his friend and fellow newspaper reporter. His eyes squinted through round, metal-framed glasses and watched the ball hit the facade between the first and second decks.

It was the fourth inning of game one of the World Series. Big Ted Kluszewski's homer had put the White Sox ahead 11 to 0 against the National League champs, the Los Angeles Dodgers, newly moved from Brooklyn. After forty years, the World Series finally had returned to the South Side of Chicago. No championship game had been played here since a handful of Black Sox players had accepted money to throw the 1919 series. Two generations of fans had suffered deeply since, excited only by an individual player's talents and efforts.

"It's a new era," Paul said, shaking Jim's hand.

"Ted Lyons," Jim said respectfully.

"Luke Appling," Paul added, naming another Sox immortal who had played his heart out during the dry years and never starred in a World Series.

"And all those foul balls he drove pitchers crazy with," Jim said.

"Let's hear it for all the kids from the old neighborhood who used to root for the Yankees," Paul said.

Jim accommodated with that most blatant of all derisive sounds, a razzberry, and thrust his fist defiantly in the air.

"You got to believe!" Paul said, panting. "You got to! That's what it's all about."

"Paul, I don't got to believe," Jim mumbled. But, looking at Paul's baseball cap, he was glad he had mouthed the words. The cap covered baldness, the results of radiation being used to treat cancer. He did not want to confront his lifelong friend.

The White Sox had won that game, then had lost the series. Paul had promised he would be around to see the White Sox play in another World Series and win. He had tried, living nine years more. The team had not come through. Paul Kowalski had wasted to nothingness from cancer on the last day of July seven weeks ago.

Jim had been cleaning out Paul's desk in the newsroom when he discovered the World Series stub. The desk was neat and full of painful memories. Paul had put his matters in order before he died, at least most of them. But to Jim, Paul had died seemingly unaware that he had left a matter unsettled with his best friend.

"Damn you, Paul." Jim's throat was dry. "You're the one who should still be around. You're the one who believed in the fairness of it all. You had to go and leave me."

"Damn it, Paul," he said, loud enough to be heard by the assistant city editor, who whirled around on his green-leather stub of a chair and arched his eyebrows.

The bank of the Sanitary and Ship Canal

"You know everything about the D.P., don't you, Eddie?" Junior asked.

The response, a reward for having asked the question, was a slight movement in the muscles around Eddie's mouth.

"Gee," Junior said. "I remember the first time you told me that your boss was a corporal in the Polish army, not a sergeant like he always says he was. But you still call the old D.P. 'Sarge,' don't you, Eddie?"

Eddie had a daily surprise for Junior, preceded always by this ritual conversation. They were discussing the man they always talked about, Eddie's boss at the cardboard factory.

"Tell me again how he always repeats everything," Junior pleaded.

With a false depth to his voice, Eddie began to imitate his boss. "'Eddie,' he say, 'You not understand, so Sarge show you.

Eddie, you good boy but you not understand. Sarge show you.' "

"D.P. really calls you a 'good boy'?"

"Sarge say, 'Eddie, you good boy. You good boy, Eddie.' "

"Eddie, you imitate him so good. Tell me about the war again," Junior begged.

"War very bad. Sarge not want to talk about war. Sarge blow up German tank. Sarge lose daughter. Sarge kill Nazi colonel who take her. Sarge not want to talk about war."

"A colonel, huh, Eddie?"

"Actually, only a major."

"Yah."

"Sarge shoot major who take daughter," Eddie mocked. "He's such a D.P.!"

"Sarge is D.P., all right," Eddie continued. "It's alias Corporal Dennis Pulaski. Even his initials are D.P. Do you think he had those initials tattooed on him in the D.P. camp?"

"Gee, Eddie, to hear the kids who got them displaced persons as parents tell about it, D.P.'s must be the most ignorant people in the world," Junior offered.

"Naw," Eddie countered sternly, unwilling to cede that anyone's parent was worse than his old man. "Not the D.P.'s. It's the cops who are the dumbest people in the world. Just remember that."

"So, Eddie, show me the surprise," Junior begged.

"Not yet."

"Then tell more about D.P." Junior said. "Tell what he says about the bad people."

"During war, many bad people. They take things. Nazis. Russians. Polski. Even Americans, they take things."

"They 'take things', huh?"

"Even daughter's tiny babushka that Sarge save."

"Eddie, ya know I don't like that part of the story. Please don't tell about the babushka."

"You want the surprise? First you got to hear about the babushka. You got no steel. You're soft like Silly Putty. You're nothing." Eddie spoke in a cold voice.

"O.K., Eddie. I'm sorry. O.K.? All right."

"Don't tell me all the time you're sorry. It makes me sick. I'll tell you the story anyway, even though you don't deserve it. The babushka belonged to D.P.'s little daughter."

"I remember that part of the story," Junior said, his voice becoming a falsetto. "Sarge save it. German soldier learn about it and he grab the babushka and throw it down an outhouse hole. Sarge go in after it."

Junior suddenly stopped.

Eddie continued, "But Sarge not find it. Soldier bring other soldiers and they laugh. They not understand. They laugh and they laugh and they bring other soldiers to see D.P. covered with shit."

Junior felt the softness inside himself that Eddie had accused him of. He managed an embarrassed smile.

"So, Eddie," Junior begged, "What did the bad people steal from D.P. today?"

"People bad. They steal all time from Sarge. America no better than Poland. They steal something every day. You see, Sarge gonna catch them."

"What did they steal?" Junior asked.

"The bad people stole a spark plug from D.P.'s car."

Eddie pulled a spark plug out of his pocket, smiled at it and handed it to Junior, who nodded to Eddie to make certain it was all right to hold it. He held up Eddie's trophy and emitted high-pitched squeals of laughter. Junior bent down and then back up and guffawed louder. Eddie took the spark plug back abruptly and just as suddenly skimmed it across the water to the middle of the canal, where it sank to join the dozens of other items he had taken from his boss on earlier days.

The game was over.

"You good boy, Eddie," Junior said, patting his companion's arm.

"Don't ever touch me," Eddie commanded.

"O.K., O.K."

"I only wish he still had that damned babushka."

"You wouldn't take that, would you, Eddie?" Junior blurted out.

Pushed neatly into the corner of Paul's drawer was a letter addressed to the "Author of the article about Resurrection Mary." That had been Paul. Jim had read the article at the time and now could not remember whether or not he had finished reading it. Stapled to the envelope was a note from his dead friend.

"Jim, this is for you when you clean out my desk."

Rooney took the hand-written letter from its envelope:

"Dear Mr. Kowalski,

"I saw her. I had never read nor heard of Resurrection Mary before I saw her. When I read your article, it settled many questions I had asked myself since seeing the beautiful blonde young lady in a long, white gown with a cape, the thin material of the gown flowing softly in the wind and her beautiful hair blowing away from her face. Here's the story and, believe me, I am of sound mind. I SAW HER.

"My husband and I dance quite frequently at the Willowbrook Ballroom in Willow Springs. When we go, we drive west on 95th Street to the cemetery on the corner of Flavin Road. There didn't used to be a big fence or gates around it. At the corner we turned right on Flavin Road to get to Willow Springs. Just as we turned that corner—walking toward us was this beautiful girl with a gown of a thin, chiffon-like material and long blonde hair blowing in the wind.

"My husband was driving and my son was sitting in the front seat beside him. I was sitting in the back seat behind my son. Both my son and I had a full view. My husband's attention was on driving. I asked, 'What is a beautiful young lady doing walking down this dark road and by a cemetery at this hour of the night. Did someone drop her off here or put her out of the car?' I kept looking as we drove on down Flavin Road, turning my head as we passed her and then gazing out through the back window. I worried about her walking alone on that lonely road. And as I looked she was there no more.

"I said, 'She's disappeared quick as a wink.' My husband said he thought she might have run into the woods, but my son and I agreed that she just vanished right in front of our eyes. I have never forgotten her. She was the prettiest thing I have seen. Ever so often, she comes in front of my eyes and I try to get some answers of my own. When I read about Resurrection Mary, I felt I too have seen her. I feel ever so strongly that it was her.

"I look for her when we go that way. Maybe some evening, when I least expect it, she'll be there, walking down that road. I have no fear. To me, she is something precious, whoever or whatever she is. She won't hurt anyone. To her, I say, 'God bless you.' I hope I will be blessed by being able to see her once more even if she disappears again right in front of my eyes.

"This letter is true, and I am of sound mind and so is my son. He is able to back my story.

"She was there."

Ruth D., Matteson.

At the end of the letter in Paul's handwriting were the words, "Jim, check her out. Check out Resurrection Mary."

Jim read the letter a second time.

"A chemical balance in the body," Jim thought. "That's why some people are believers. I don't have it."

Jim's religion was being a newspaper reporter. His catechism was the motto on his desk, culled from an editor at the City News Bureau where he had apprenticed. It said, "If your mother says she loves you, check it out."

Jim Rooney checked out his facts, just as he tested his relationships. No matter what he tried, he did not have the salve of belief with which to meet the unknown and the difficult. Many around him, especially Paul, did have it.

"It probably means I'll die kicking and screaming, not serenely as Paul did," he said to himself.

He realized now that his friend had understood. In the letter Paul was making a last hopeful effort to awaken Jim's ability to probe the possibility of faith.

The remembrance of their relationship spread from his heart through the rest of his being, loosening the lump in his throat.

"Paul," he said, smiling, "If you wanted to convert me with this letter, you won't succeed. I can't believe in spirits. If I could, it would be the continuing existence of your soul that I'd believe in."

∾

CHAPTER ONE

☙

Archer Avenue in the southwest suburbs of Chicago

Late Friday evening

The misty night had taken hold of Archer Avenue. The wild, wooded stretches, just southwest of Chicago, between Resurrection and St. James Sag cemeteries await a frightening nocturnal visitor—an ancient, black hearse drawn by four charging horses. It appears from nowhere, racing through the dark. The ghostly beams of its two gas lamps flicker on overhanging tree branches and cut the eerie mist.

The sepulchral apparition's shiny wooden frame is of the blackest oak. Its glass sides shimmer in what little moonlight there is, exposing in outline the white coffin of a child. There is no driver. Its horses rush forward, like panting creatures trying to escape hell itself.

The terror of the hearse rips a hole in the soul of everyone who ever has encountered it. Some Southwest suburb residents have seen this hearse, other have felt its presence, and many more believe in it.

No breeze stirs. The birds, frogs, and crickets are silent in the face of the deeper night.

Another vehicle, equally black, a high-finned Cadillac, with only parking lights on, roars toward the on-coming apparition.

Archer Avenue is a two-lane highway. It is paved but does not seem to be, as nature has encroached, surrounding it with bushes, tree limbs, and leaves. Few late-summer leaves have fallen as the foliage crowds the little-used highway that sees even less traffic at night. Built in the 1830s along the route of the planned Illinois and Michigan Canal, Archer Avenue had become a trail of sweat and disappointment during those years. Irish canal workers trudged out from Bridgeport, then a suburb, to find out whether there would be work that day on the financially-troubled canal. Mostly there was not.

Many of these Irish canalers are buried in no-longer identifiable gravesites in St. James Sag Cemetery. The church and its cemetery sit on a high bluff that overlooks Archer Avenue on one side and a majestic slough and valley once sacred to prehistoric Indians on the other.

The city's ghosts, the troubled spirits of the dead some say, have claimed this wild stretch of highway. Southwest Siders will tell of events that happened almost a hundred years ago and have been reenacted since. They will also tell of a strange series of events that began on this September night in 1968.

On this night, a brown four-door 1962 Dodge convertible is parked half-hidden in the wooded start of a road off Archer Avenue. This "making out" spot, known as the "the turn-around," is a mile and a half northeast of St. James Sag Church and Cemetery. A desolate wilderness area with its scraggly-armed trees and hilly terrain, it appears more akin to the isolated woods of Southern Illinois or forgotten parts of West Virginia than to the human bustle of Chicago, a handful of miles northeast.

The Dodge, with its chrome strips and hubcaps, contrasts with the softness of the grasses, bushes, and trees, which seem to twitch in the windless night. The air is crisp. Away from the glow of the city and the bright new vapor lamps that Mayor Richard J. Daley has installed on Chicago streets, Archer Avenue seems unusually dark. The moon, when it appears through a break in the dark clouds, outlines forms in the night. In the lore of the turn-around, one legend tells of Al Capone's gang dumping bodies off here during the 1920s. In another story, Capone's men held machine gun practice here. Such tales abound in the area.

Janice O'Leary, scrunched in the corner of the back seat of the Dodge, felt Eddie Wolinski's warm hand slide back and forth on her goose-pimpled thigh. Pursing tight her lips, she decided with rigid determination to let Eddie pursue his course. And, darn it, she was somehow going to enjoy this. Twice she has started to stop him and actually slowed down Eddie's hand long enough for her to take the deep breath she needed. His fingers reached up to pull at her panties.

A shriek. It was Janice's. Her electric scream split the still night air surrounding the car. The couple entwined in the front seat started up in astonishment.

Eddie flushed with anger and trembled with an impulse to hurt. He has planned this encounter carefully, and Janice has ruined it with her scream.

She screamed, he knew with full fury and certainty, because she did not want to go along and is willing to reject him. She had the audacity to want to take control away from Eddie Wolinski.

"Damn it, she never did want to do it," he cursed in his head. "Now I won't ever be able to get myself going. Damn girl. I will kill her."

"I saw it," Janice blurted out.

"What did you see?" Eddie yelled at her. "What in hell did you think you saw?"

"The hearse, I...It was awful. Terrifying. I, I saw it go by..."

Eddie responded with a hard slap on the left side of her face. "No goddamn hearse went by! That was a car with only its parking lights on. Right, you guys up there in front? You guys up front, you paying attention to me?"

Junior Grady, looking back at Janice in the rear seat, filled himself with Eddie's angry exasperation. He pulled a pack of Chesterfields out from his pocket.

"Chrissake, you stupid chick," Junior added to his buddy's comment. "How dare you embarrass Eddie?"

"I'm sorry," Janice apologized, touching her sore cheek.

"You know what, Janice," Junior said, lighting a cigarette and pushing aside Nancy's dress. "That may have been your damn hearse, but it squealed when it went around the bend. Tell me how some ancient goddamn hearse is going to squeal like a car that needs a brake job. The hearse of Archer Avenue needs a goddamn brake job!"

Janice curled up, arching her arm over her head as though expecting to have to ward off another blow from Eddie.

"They're right," she conceded to herself. "It probably was a car."

She flushed.

"It was so terrifying. I was so sure." Her pride would have her refuse to give in, but this was Eddie with whom she was dealing.

"It was not a car. I saw Resurrection Mary's hearse. I'm sorry I saw it."

Eddie, the heat of his anger continuing to replace that of his passion, formed a fist with his hand.

"We are going to find that car," he ordered.

The two boys had an unspoken understanding. By the time Eddie mentioned a course of action, Junior had started doing it, Eddie alone determining the direction.

The Dodge careened onto the highway and thumped onto the cement roadbed, its headlights flashing on. The racing tires shrieked through the night, sending off a message of wild anger.

It was not a hearse that Janice had heard that September night in 1968. It was the 1959 Cadillac which had sped northeast on Archer Avenue with its parking lights on. The car had needed a brake job, as the sheriff's inspection of the vehicle would report later.

As Gary McDonough's anger had become intense, he had found a way to express it. It was his Cadillac.

His father had called him a bum and told him to get out of the house. It was his old man who was the bum, he said to himself for the twentieth time.

"Gary McDonough ain't going to take just any job. I'm ain't going to accept one until it's right, very right. And nobody is going to make me."

Turning the ignition on had felt as though he were taking

the reins of charging horses in his hands.

"Thank God for this goddamned car," he said. His pent-up frustration with his father turned into a snarl and an angry determination not to turn the stupid headlights on.

Gary knew this stretch of Archer Avenue. For awhile, the car almost steered itself. He focused on the dark in front of him. He did not know what it was that seemed to be rushing at him in the night with even less light cutting the mist than the parking lights on his own vehicle. He swerved hard to avoid hitting it head on. It was the last thing Gary ever did.

Ten minutes later

Janice O'Leary never before had been present when someone had just died. She knew of only one member of her family who had. Her mother had witnessed the death of her great aunt, a pious woman who had attended Mass daily and who had visited such religious shrines as Lourdes, Fatima and Guadaloupe. Her mother said that, immediately after her aunt died, her spirit had hovered in the form of a light mist over her body for a few seconds and it then had evaporated.

Janice noted such a cloud over the hood of the wrecked Cadillac.

"Look, just over the hood," she said, "It's somebody's soul."

"Radiator steam," Eddie snapped.

The wreck did smell of boiling anti-freeze and burning oil, but the image of a mist hovering above the car was clearly impressed in Janice's mind and locked deep in her memory. She knew immediately that someone had died in the wreck. Another car, driven by an off-duty deputy sheriff, already had stopped. He had called for an ambulance.

The road showed two bizarre skidmarks. Junior noticed that the black tracks veered quickly to the right; the driver had tried to avoid something coming directly at him. They were wobbly, showing the high speed at which the car had been traveling.

The skidmarks were there. The bushes had been knocked down. The metal of the car was twisted against the trunk of a tree. The windshield was smashed. But none of these frightening details seemed in the same world of reality as the brutal fact that the mangled body of 20-year-old Gary McDonough lay 25 feet from the car where it been thrown by the impact of the crash. A sense of death did not capture the others as it did Janice. Junior said later he expected the body to get up and walk away or at least to cry out how much it hurt to be gashed open and bleeding. Not Janice. To her, the boy was as dead as anyone she had ever seen in a funeral parlor.

"Stand back. I'm in charge here," the deputy sheriff said with authority and a touch of belligerence. "You young people, get back. One of your kind already showed he doesn't know how to be responsible tonight."

Eddie snorted. Junior quickly intercepted him, knowing that if Eddie's anger got the better of him he would take on the deputy sheriff right then and there. The man was among those people Eddie loathed most in life, policemen.

"Eddie, this idiot doesn't know what he's talking about," Junior protested in a low voice.

"I knew this kid, not his name, but I knew him," Eddie lied. "Don't knock him. He's dead. Don't talk like that about him."

The deputy, who had enough problems with his own son, was not in any mood to back down. After he had this cleaned up, he was going home to give his 17-year-old son, Brian, a stern lecture. He might as well start with these kids. He was angry that this kid had killed himself. He himself had done some wild things when he was 18, and he knew how stupid teenagers can be.

"One smart word out of your mouth," he threatened, "and I'm going to take you all in."

Junior knew that, long after the deputy had left this scene, Eddie would still be there. There was no way he was going to back down when somebody tried to make him accept authority the way this deputy just had. Junior, in such situations, immediately looked out to protect Eddie and himself from Eddie's bullheadedness.

"What can go wrong? What can cause us trouble? Where's it going to hit the fan?" Junior asked himself.

"The girls. It's past curfew," he whispered to Eddie.

"So, get 'em out of here," Eddie snapped.

"I can't believe this," Nancy said.

Janice took in what was happening, all of it. Death was real. Eddie's reaction was, too.

"I'm alone, so very much alone." She choked to herself, "If I fall, I'll just keep falling. Nobody, nothing would catch me."

For Janice, it was as though she had died before and she were very afraid of it.

"Dear, don't worry. You don't just die," her mother once had reassured her. "You die from something. There is a cause, and the doctors can explain it. Usually you get very, very sick first."

How reassuring that had been! But Janice now saw before her the body of this boy who had not been sick first. The logic that her mother had promised her about death was missing from this accident scene. She thought of the hearse, but only for a second.

Junior was talking. "You girls are under age, and it's past curfew and this cop is going to make it rough before he is through," he said, making no reference to Eddie's determination to outdo the deputy. "I'll drive you down the road a little and park you out of the way."

"Under age," Janice murmured to herself, recalling what they had been doing ten minutes earlier. That memory made her even more frightened and more lonely.

"What a jump from making out to death, with Eddie trying to pick a fight with the cop on top of it all!" She fought back tears.

She wanted desperately to leave. She didn't and wouldn't think of saying so. She would merely be yelled at. She was a girl, Eddie's girl. It wasn't for her to say where they were going or when, especially in a situation like this.

Eddie stayed there, standing his ground, staring with

unabated hatred at the deputy sheriff. Junior drove the Dodge and the two girls a quarter of mile southwest on Archer Avenue, well out of sight of the cars that were stopping to view the accident scene. The sound of an approaching ambulance or police car, they were not certain which, indicated that one more vehicle was speeding down Archer Avenue in an unnecessary hurry.

Janice and Nancy sat in the car, expressionless, preparing for the long wait. Each thought of her parents and how, this time, she would explain the awfully late hour she would arrive home. Neither shared the stories passing through her thoughts, wondering if her parents might buy it. Janice lacked Nancy's easy ability to lie. Nancy could talk for an hour and a half and give detail after detail of something she made up out of her head. Janice was more literal. It hurt her to lie. It was a violation of herself.

The two waited in the car, but not entirely in silence. They made small noises, more groans than words. Janice's preoccupation with her excuse evaporated. The flood of images of the wrecked car and the dead young man seeped into her consciousness and almost overwhelmed her.

Nancy lit a cigarette. Janice did not smoke. Actually, cigarette smoke nauseated her. Janice never had been this nervous before, not even sitting in the principal's office, certain that the nun was going to suspend her.

"Nan," she said, finally, "Give me a smoke."

"You? You'll get sick....Here," Nancy said, handing her a cigarette, not even bothering to hold it back.

Janice took the cigarette, pursed it in her lips and accepted a light from Nancy's lighter. The first puff tasted awful but felt good. It was something to do. And, God, she needed that. Janice inhaled the way Eddie once had shown her. She began to feel the bottom of her stomach and then her esophagus, then her throat and then her stomach again. She was going to throw up. Janice pushed open the door and rushed into the woods until she came to a large oak. She stood behind it and felt the rush of partially digested food come from her mouth with a force she could not believe. Then it was over. She was embarrassed, more so than when she had vomited from drinking too much. She hesitated to return to the car. Nancy had warned her. What was there to go back to?

Janice felt the loneliness again.

Then, she heard a sound that began softly, a little louder than the rustle of the leaves. It was something surrounding her. It was music, strong resonant male voices. She thought she recognized the music. It was chant, a Gregorian chant. She had heard it before at Holy Name Cathedral when she went there once with her mother, and on another occasion with her eighth grade class. It was getting louder, and she did not understand. It was coming from the woods around her, and she did not know how or why. Janice was scared—lonely scared. She ran back to the car.

Nancy yelled at her, "Where have you been? What is that sound, that music?"

"I don't know, Nan. Let's get Eddie."

They ran, stumbling in the darkness.

Eddie was still belligerent, but the deputy had become involved in the accident and seemed no longer aware of his existence. Eddie was glad for an excuse to leave.

"That pig!" he said, as he retreated. "I'll show him some-day. I have his name."

"What do you mean that you threw up and then you heard music?" he challenged, diverting his anger toward his girlfriend.

"We both heard music," Janice said, apologetically. "I'm the only one who threw up. Come back to the car. You'll hear it, too."

All four stood at the car listening.

"Hey, that sounds like when our pastor was buried," Junior said.

"Let's find out where it's coming from," Janice said with an independence that she did not know she had.

"No, I'm leaving," Eddie said flatly. He was the leader, and they, the followers. No one questioned his decision.

"Hey," Junior said. "I think I know what words they were singing."

"I thought it was Latin," Eddie challenged. He did not believe Junior or anyone else ever knew more about anything than he did.

"I didn't say I knew what they mean, just that the words were 'di-es eyrie, di-es ill-a.'"

"I don't ever want to know what those words mean," Eddie Wolinski said.

∽

CHAPTER TWO

ↄ

11:30 P.M., Friday

"Check her out."

The words seem to whistle softly from Jim's mouth as he took one last look through the drawers of Paul's desk.

"Check out Resurrection Mary." He wanted to think of her rather than of his immediate assignment.

Paul was dead. That fact intruded constantly into Jim's thinking, thinking already shaken by a new loneliness in his life. The connections he had both with Beth, his wife, and with his daughter had also been undone recently. There was no one else to talk with or with whom to share his life. He himself was his only daily test of reality.

"This is for you," Paul had written. The challenge was cryptic. He was gone, no longer someone with whom Jim could argue, disagree, or laugh. But he was there, somehow Paul was still there. If Jim had tested Paul's continued existence with a question, his mind would have denied it. Because his feelings did not want to ask questions, Jim was free to respond to Paul's legacy, Resurrection Mary, no matter how inexorably his logic told him it was ridiculous.

In the last few weeks Paul somehow had become intermittently present to him. And, when he was there, it was as though he were right by his ear. The feeling was both strange and familiar. Jim wondered at his own response. It was, and he struggled for a word, "tenderness." Perhaps, he reflected, it was a carryover from his feeling of their last hours together and of Paul's efforts to whisper one last joke, one last tease, to Jim. Death had broken a dam that held back his emotions.

Resurrection Mary was beginning to be the center of his

attention. Her story, an unfinished communication between them, was an inheritance Jim could shape and use to meet his own immediate needs and purposes. Minimally, pursuing the story might be a distraction. That would be enough.

"Check her out."

An idea and a plan leaped across the gap. The inspiration was Paul's; the course of action would be Jim's.

Something unusual seemed to be awaiting him, as though Paul had promised that it would. Jim would not let his ingrained skepticism get in the way of it.

The time for Jim to start his checking was now. It was always "now" with him. He would start by pulling and reading all the clippings in the newspaper's reference room on Resurrection Mary.

"I miss him, too," a voice said. Jim looked up at the assistant sports editor, who was passing the desk on his way out. "He helped me stop drinking. I'll tell you about it sometime."

"He helped a lot of people," Jim answered. "He left me his stubs from the 1959 World Series. He promised me he'd live to see the Sox win one, the son of a gun."

"Paul didn't break many promises."

"Let me tell you something," Jim said, "Our buddy is still trying to help me. I'll tell you about that when you tell me about the drinking."

"Sure. Good night, anyway."

The interlude made Jim aware of feeling hooked onto a conveyor belt pulled by his own compulsion.

Busby was on a long call with a deputy sheriff friend. It gave Jim time to go to the reference room. In the clipping files, he knew, accounts of people and events were preserved—colorfully, if not always accurately. The one reference clerk on duty was busy elsewhere when Jim pulled the file.

The old biographical clippings kept by the newspaper were in dusty yellow, business-size manila envelopes. Files on deceased people had the word "dead" typed in unusually large letters on the outside. The one Jim held was an exception. That word which would have been appropriate was omitted.

Two words were imprinted on it by the reference room's special typewriter—"Resurrection Mary." Unlike other dead people in the clipping file of a major Chicago newspaper, the city's most famous ghost was not listed as deceased.

Carefully Jim slid the clippings out of the envelope. Some had yellowed. Others were still white.

"Rooney, did you cover that thing in Lincoln Park a couple of weeks ago?" a voice asked.

"What?"

"Did you cover the riots in Lincoln Park a few weeks ago?"

The question had come from the reference room clerk.

"Yes, I did."

"Good," the young man asked. "Nobody, and I mean nobody on the night shift can remember which day it was."

"It was Monday, August 26," Jim answered, adding to himself, "God, how quick they forget!"

Jim had not forgotten.

He had gotten his head broken open two weeks earlier and a fellow employee had to ask him if he had been in Lincoln Park. Just another part of the disillusionment that had started in his life that night!

God, if he could only forget! The protestors against the Vietnam War and President Lyndon Johnson's role in it had gathered in Chicago to use the Democratic National Convention as their stage. It was a news story heard around the world and Jim had been on the street, in the midst of it. Monday, August 26, had given Jim a bunch of ugly memories. He tramped around the spacious, gently rolling and wooded Lincoln Park early in the evening as Allen Ginsburg and his Yippies chanted their monotonous buddhist chant, "Ommmmmm." Young anti-war activists sat, camped and held hands. They painted posters and spoke to each other in serious voices. There was an electricity, but little that was newsworthy. Jim had held his glasses steady to read a flyer that he had picked up:

yippee!
Lincoln Park
Vote pig in '68

Free motel
Come sleep with us
Revolution towards a free society: Yippie!
By a Yippie

1. An immediate end to the war in Viet Nam.
2. Immediate freedom for Huey Newton of the Black Panthers and all other black people. Adoption of the community control concept in our ghetto areas.
3. The legalization of marijuana and all other psychedelic drugs.

There had been other points, but Jim did not take any of them very seriously. He was queasy about such protestors. They were very different people from any he had ever encountered before, even as a reporter in Chicago. They seemed to try to be different. That was a violation of one of his most basic instincts. They were the crazies his fellow journalists smirked about. "Loonies" was his own favorite word.

Lincoln Park was crowded with a mix of them: yippies, protestors, and flower children as well as curious young people, priests, and ministers. The police had talked of clearing the park. Mayor Daley had been adamant about enforcing an 11 o'clock curfew there. Jim did not believe that the young people would leave Lincoln Park, nor did he see any problem with them staying. He expected a nose-to-nose confrontation, with a lot of rhetoric and confused negotiation. Such confrontations, for years, had been his beat, with people who used Dr. Martin Luther King's passive resistance in protesting segregation, the war, and school issues. Jim thought he knew the Chicago Police Department. He was not prepared for what exploded.

With their blue uniforms and riot helmets, the police came out from the trees in a fast wave, billyclubs swinging. Many had deliberately removed badges, nameplates and unit insignias—to be anonymous as they angrily attacked and vented their contempt and fury. Their hard-driving clubs not only targeted young people who looked like demonstrators, but also singled out photographers, priests, and reporters.

"Damn it to hell," Jim had cried out in shock and disbelief, as well as protest. Like others, he had been wearing clear press identification. The cop, whose club hit him on the shoulders and back, rushed Jim from behind after he had started to run. The blows cracked and hurt, ending with a slashing blow to the back of his skull that brought blood and knocked him to his knees.

Until that final hit, Jim had no trouble with the system or with the police as respected defenders of it. But how and why this? Fortunately, he got more of a headache than a concussion. Seventeen newsmen and photographers filled the emergency room at nearby Henrotin hospital.

Jim's trust in newspaper editors lasted only a few days longer. At first, the editors protested loudly and stridently against the brutal behavior of the police. Then, in midstream, they met with the Chicago Superintendent of Police. Things changed. The editors downplayed reporting of police violence and gave room "to Daley's side." That meant, essentially, reprinting extracts from a "soft" Walter Cronkite exclusive interview with the Mayor of Chicago.

It is hard to ask "why?" and not want to do something, Jim had concluded. He measured where he had put his faith. When he was a child, he had placed it with his parents—and they had gotten divorced. They had never argued in front of him. They did not think he could handle it. That was a bitter pill. They never realized it was their lack of trust in him, not the divorce, that was the issue. He still saw them occasionally these days, but only the shell of his relationship with either was left.

Now his loneliness was total. His divorce, Paul's death, and the violence of the convention all had created vacuums deep within him. He wanted to run away, quit, leave town, bury himself. He did not know why he did not.

He decided to focus on the one problem that might just be solveable, working nights at the paper. The night staff on the paper represented the old school of Chicago journalism, a throw-back to the reporters of the 1920s, whose reputations had been built on a good story, gotten any way available.

Jim considered himself less colorful than many of his colleagues on the paper. For their part, they respected him enough to want to make him over to their image. They knew he had a skeptical strain; they wanted to bring it out and let it flower as it had in them. He had lost the battle to keep his family together. No, he would not lose this one with his fellow journalists.

Paul's letter about Resurrection Mary could become part of Jim's plan to get off nights. He would attain greater freedom from the people on the City Desk if he were a columnist.

"If only I could sell the front office on a four-day-a-week column about Chicago's neighborhoods," he told himself.

He knew what his first column would be. He would accept Paul's challenge. He would write about the ghost of the young woman who haunted the Southwest Side. It had been Paul's legacy to him. He somehow would find the original incident that triggered the Resurrection Mary legend or else would establish, as he suspected, that it could not be true and obviously had been fabricated. Either way, the search itself would provide a good story.

The reference room extension phone rang. It was the voice of Busby, the bulbous-faced night city editor. "Rooney, are you with us tonight? We have a little story we'd like you to write for this newspaper."

Busby—no one used his first name anymore—had mellowed.

"That's a gross understatement," said one rewrite-man who had known Busby for half of the fifty years he had been on the paper.

He looked like a callow Alfred Hitchcock. His pallid complexion seemed to have avoided any contact with sunlight for years. His jowls often twisted into an impish grin. Busby, now in his seventies, had started as a copyboy during World War I. Stories had it—and Busby was not above starting legends about himself—that during his career, he had helped solve five major murders in Chicago. *Time* magazine had called him "the last of the bulldog reporters." On the telephone he was unbelievably creative, usually establishing a new identity with each call. He expected everyone who worked under him to participate eagerly in such seat-of-the-pants journalistic flights.

Rooney's approach was different from Busby's. He was skeptical, but not cynical.

Busby had softened. He no longer fried each new reporter on the griddle of his sarcasm or took pleasure in giving them imporssible assignments. Still, for his own reasons, he chose Jim Rooney as a foil. A light glowed in Busby's beady eyes as his comments hung in the air, dripping with sardonic humor. Actually this was the treatment Busby reserved for those young reporters he liked. Those whom he did not like, he grunted at or ignored altogether. Busby wanted to convert Rooney to his sardonic view of reality. Jim knew that.

Jim had made a mistake. He mumbled "no" on the phone at Busby. He had not meant for the older man to hear him, but he had. Busby loved such a challenge. He sat back, laughed and bellowed at Jim. "Rooney, get in here now!"

A day-side reporter polishing up a story and the two other rewritemen on the night shift each gave Jim a sympathetic glance when he appeared in the City Room.

"Mr. Rooney, a young man died tonight. Tomorrow, this newspaper is going to tell its readers that he is no longer with us. I thought you might be willing to help this paper do that. But, you said, 'no.' Do you have somebody you were rendez-vousing with in the reference room?" The temptation to an-swer "Resurrection Mary" was given a quick pass by the reporter.

"Tonight," Busby continued, "a young man was killed out on Archer Avenue. I spoke with a deputy sheriff. Drag-racing might be involved. There were other young people. He didn't talk to them, but he got their license plate numbers. We followed up and got the address. I want you to go and talk to these kids at home right now."

That was Busby's twist. If there were ever a reporter in the United States who believed a story could be gotten over the telephone, it was Chicago's own Busby. He operated the phone in the middle of the night like a master puppeteer, calling people at will, waking them up and putting them on his stage. But this time he was sending Rooney out to knock on some door, in the middle of the night, to ask the parents if he could talk to their kids and see if they had been drag-racing when a young man was killed.

Jim bristled. He would do it, but he was more determined than ever to escape the night side.

As Jim left the office, he committed a journalistic sin. He took Resurrection Mary with him. He removed her from the building in her dusty yellow envelope. He would stop somewhere and have coffee far away from Busby and read about the ghost named after a cemetery on Archer Avenue.

Just past midnight, Saturday morning

Jim knew one certainty. If those kids had been drag-racing and a friend of theirs had been killed, they would not be home yet. Even if they hadn't been drag-racing, they had witnessed the death of the other kid, according to the story Busby had told him. Under the circumstances, they would not have gone home right away. They would have stayed together and gone some place to talk about it, to deal with it.

Another issue was involved. Jim did not want to knock on the door and have to explain his mission to some privacy-conscious parent. Jim knew about Southwest Side parents. He had two of his own. Such parents protect their children against anyone from the outside. They could see their kid do something and then deny it. That protection is total, as any desk sergeant will tell you.

"My kid didn't do it," they would say. "He wouldn't do something like that. He's a good boy."

Parents in other areas might take a similar position. But the length of time parents on the Southwest Side of Chicago hold to the story astounds outsiders. Even those whose sons are serving 10 to 20 years in the penitentiary are emphatic that their kid never did anything wrong in his life. The offenses they deny can range from sassing a teacher to murder.

"Not my kid."

On the other hand, inside the home, the kid is judged guilty summarily and punished severely. Guilt inside the home is presumed with the same certainty it is denied outside. Demands are strong and discipline is rigid. Parents assume all responsibility for punishments and administer them while denying to outsiders that any offense had been committed.

A reporter such as Rooney represented the outside as much as the police might. He had to find the kids themselves or simply report back that no one had been home. Jim would not waste his time and suffer the aggravation of knocking on someone's door just to satisfy the whims of old Busby.

"Where would they be? Where should I go?" he asked himself.

He drove "old Betsy," his olive, 1956 Chevy out to the Southwest Side, choosing a slower route to give himself time to mull the situation over. Instead of taking the Southwest Expressway, he chose Archer Avenue, parallel but just south of the expressway. Inside the city limits Archer avenue is mile after mile of small businesses, remnants of the dream of postwar expansion.

The Southwest Side had changed little since he was a teenager. O'Hare International Airport, northwest of the city, after it opened in 1956, had taken the heavy flight traffic away from the Southwest Side's Midway Airport. Some motels and undeveloped lots already were beginning to deteriorate from lack of upkeep.

The Southwest Expressway had diverted a substantial number of cars from Archer Avenue. At election time, politicians still talked of extending the elevated train route out this way, but Jim did not think it would ever be built.

The Southwest Side was a comfortable womb for Jim Rooney and 300,000 other Chicagoans, many of them a mixture of eastern European and Irish, as he was. Its boundaries were precise. The northern boundary was the Southwest Expressway, later to be renamed the Stevenson Expressway.

The eastern boundary was State Street; the western, the city limits along Harlem Avenue; the southern boundary jogged, at times running as far south as 79th Street. That womb also could be a prison, as Jim well knew. This fact people from the outside perhaps could see more easily than a person raised here.

Sometimes Jim wondered: womb or prison—or are they the same?

"Such heavy thinking!" he criticized himself. "Where could those kids be? Sliders," he suddenly thought. "Yes, that's the answer—sliders!" Jim grinned.

Someone from Rogers Park, north along the lake, once had asked Paul and Jim what was the most characteristic nuance they could think of to describe the Southwest Side. Jim's immediate response had been "sliders," an answer with which Paul happily agreed.

A "slider" is a White Castle hamburger. The term, Jim had always thought, referred in particular to the hamburgers sold at the White Castle either on the northwest corner of Archer and Kedzie Avenues or the one at Ogden and Harlem Avenues. "Slider" was not a word printed anywhere or advertised in any way. But those who lived in the area simply knew what it meant. A new chain, McDonald's, was making inroads, but probably could do better in Bangkok, Thailand, than on the Southwest Side of Chicago, even though the original McDonald's was in Des Plaines, a northwest suburb of Chicago.

McDonald's had golden arches and big signs telling how many million hamburgers it had sold. White Castle's white-marbled little fast-food restaurants out-generationed McDonald's. Jim felt he might find the young people and their 1959 Dodge, license 342-789, at the White Castle at Ogden and Harlem. It was intuition. He was confident about his hunch.

"You know your territory and you know your people," Jim told himself. He was also aware that there were few other places open this late at night where teenagers could go.

The restaurant at Ogden and Harlem was a calm white

island with a substantial parking lot. It seemed like a port in a storm as heavy truck traffic rumbled past. When Jim had gone to school, he had waited for his bus here. He knew every inch of the terrain and very little of it had changed. When he pulled into the parking lot, however, there was no Dodge. They were not here.

"But they will be." He was convinced.

He decided to wait. He got out of the car and muttered sternly to himself, "...only coffee. Your stomach can't take those greasy little sliders." He also knew it was a resolution he wouldn't keep.

Only as he started to open the door to the White Castle did he realize he had left Resurrection Mary on the front seat of his car. Jim returned to the car and picked up the envelope. He shut the door and stared at the restaurant.

"Well, Mary," he said to the envelope in his hand, "this glorified hamburger joint is as close as we common people on the Southwest Side ever get to a castle. Let's go haunt it."

℅

CHAPTER THREE

℃℃

Janice O'Leary's stare passed through the White Castle window, which captured her reflection—out onto Harlem Avenue. Eddie and Junior had left her there and returned to the scene of the accident. Nancy had been dropped off at her house.

Janice picked at a ketchup-stained carton of cold french fries, trying to find an option. But there was none. Even these fries had to be eaten. Life had to be lived. A million little things had to be done. And, then, you died. You died, but you did not escape, which is what you wanted to do but could not. Rituals you would observe and routes you would follow; but there would be no escape.

From everlasting monotony, deliver us, O Lord.

Every night for a year she had gone out to whichever hamburger drive-in was the "hangout" for her and her friends. There, they insulted each other and attacked one another—for being dumb, for being smart, for each and every way in which each one (except Eddie) was different from the others in the group.

Everybody was a "tanker," especially anyone who drank too much, which was more a virtue than a fault. The phrase was "you tanker." They might call someone "you dope" or "you freak," but such variations were rare.

The group was "the kids" and females were "the girls," a

term even women in their sixties called each other. Older women could grow out of it by being called *Babi* in Czech or *Busia* in Polish. Both mean grandmother, but even women who never had children or grandchildren often claimed the title.

Mainly kids talked about other people and complained a lot about their parents, how unfair or "out of it" they were. Parents were criticized coldly for being "too Polish," "too Irish," "too Catholic," and "too dumb." The worst insult was to call a person a "D.P." To this post-World War II generation D.P. meant "a displaced person." These people, having lost everything including their homes and often their families, made up an immigration wave that nevertheless was spared none of the opprobrium always heaped on new arrivals. Often the children of the D.P.'s joined in the vituperation, resenting that their parents had "old ways" and had not been assimilated fully.

From the sins of our children, deliver us, O Lord.

The kids griped about teachers, what "drips" and "nags" they were, about kids who were not smart enough or were too smart, were too weird or too straight, and about anyone not totally cool, not "one of us." The only totally right people were angry—rock and roll stars rebellious or rich enough to tell adults to "shove it."

Usually Eddie and the gang went for car rides, everyone, that is, except Sally Horwitz. She wanted to be begged to go along, but Eddie, whose girl she once had been, would smirk and order that no one ask her. The forest preserves nearby belonged to them, they figured, as much as their own neighborhood did. The preserves were a turf where the rules of life were freer. You could drink, be rowdier and you could carve on or destroy whatever you could find—signs, picnic tables, outhouses or rain shelters.

Convertibles were a means of torture for girls, and none wanted to ride in one, but they did. What a speeding car with no top could do to a bouffant hairdo was unbelievable and to be avoided. Hair was supremely important, unless you didn't want to look "pretty." The only acceptable style was a bouffant, hairspray-sticky beehive. During the course of one year, a female substitute teacher once mathematically determined that a girl would use a barrel of hairspray to hold her bouffant up.

Hairstyle controlled many aspects of life besides convertible-riding. In the summer, when the kids drove to the lake, they always went to the same place, Rainbow Beach. From the Southwest Side, it was the closest whites-only beach along the south shore of Lake Michigan. Rainbow was an hour and a half ride. At the beach Janice and the other girls with their glued-up hairdos never went in the water.

Boys, except for "real creeps," treated girls' hair with reverence. Even Eddie was careful, except with Sally Horwitz. A boy could be mean in teasing a girl and playing around at a swimming pool, but he would be careful not to get her hair wet. A Southwest Side boy might take a girl's virginity, but he would not muss up her hair doing it. If he did, it was said, she probably would complain more about her hair than her lost innocence.

Pranks were the chief weapon to avert boredom. The group's hero was Eddie, who was most creatively vicious in carrying off a prank, thereby relieving boredom and expressing defiance. Once Eddie took a gate off of an alley entranceway and put it on the person's front porch in such a way that it crashed through a window when the owner, answering the doorbell, opened the door. He stood and let the man swear at his figure half-hidden in the shadows.

One lady used to scream at the kids because they cut through her gangway to get to the alley. One day, Junior noticed and told Eddie she had all her teeth out and had not yet obtained false ones. That was all Eddie needed to know. He went home and got a camera and slowly paraded through the gangway. Predictably, she appeared to yell at him. Waiting until she was up close, he pulled out the camera and started snapping. Eddie posted one of the pictures on the bulletin board at the Kroger supermarket.

From the grubby clutches of fate, deliver us, O Lord.

Janice had a hobby. She had started it long before she met Eddie. It was a private and intense interest no one else knew about. She collected the newspaper reports of ghosts or supernatural phenomena in the neighborhood. To Janice, it was a secret and compelling passion. But her most interesting files were in her head. These were oral tradition of ghosts on the Southwest Side or suburbs of Chicago.

Janice never told anyone else about the ghosts. It was as though she and the ghosts belonged to a different religion, an experience with which she, as a Catholic, was familiar. Many of her classmates in high school were Protestants.

Now, even her ghosts were not enough to fill the void. Within the last year she had started to drink. Janice had been surprised about drinking. No one had told her that it would help her forget momentarily how boring life could be. But, several times she had become sick from the liquor.

"Nothing, no how, is more boring than school," was the first comment she had ever heard Eddie Wolinski make. She thought the statement was not only cool but also a bond she shared with him. She did not work at her education and received no rewards from it. She was not challenged and she did not care. School books had nothing to do with real life. The boys and girls in the books were all beautiful, were not bored, and lived only in the unreal worlds of Spanish, health science, math, and the French Revolution.

School was always there. She was a senior with the last school year just starting. Janice had to escape. She did not know if it were possible to die from boredom, but there were times when she seemed on the brink of it. She could continue to get through it day by day. That was her mother's suggestion. Her parents did not realize that Janice knew or even cared where the key to the liquor cabinet was hidden. She would just drop out of high school, get a job and take classes at night. If she did not like night school, she could take a high school equivalency test. She was 17, but looked older.

Eddie worked in a factory. He said he probably could get her a job there. Maybe even in the front office. Otherwise, she could ask around about a job as a waitress.

There was another solution. She could marry Eddie. He had not asked, but Eddie was a person who tried so hard to manipulate others that he probably could be had himself. Sometimes he hit her, but there was something comfortably familiar about him and his comments. And maybe sex as a married lady and maybe having kids would root out her boredom.

Any of her solutions, she told herself, was better than death from boredom. The problem was that she was stuck in neutral and did not seem to have enough hope even to try any of the solutions.

From the sin of Eve and Adam, of Sodom and Gomohorra, of the golden calf in the desert, of David and of Solomon, of Herod and Salome, and the sin of being bored...deliver us, O Lord.

1 A.M., Saturday

Jim had given himself several excuses for ordering the whole "bundle of sliders special." They still cost the same amount, 12 cents each, but somehow it seemed he saved money if he bought more at once instead of having to keep going back for more.

"Better to buy the bundle," Jim told himself.

He had to get something to eat. Usually about this time of night, he picked up a snack at Billy Goat's Tavern on lower Michigan Avenue.

He snapped a slider, munching it down in two bites. Opening the reference room envelope again, he flipped through the precisely cut clippings and laughed. The envelope contained a handful not only on Resurrection Mary, but also on "Typhoid Mary" and "Milkshake Mary." All three Marys probably had had separate envelopes, but space apparently had become scarce and someone had started combining different subjects.

"Milkshake Mary," one feature story clipping elaborated, was the name given to a Chicago mother of four convicted of attempting to murder her husband by feeding him milkshakes spiked with arsenic. After drinking twenty times the amount of arsenic normally tolerated by the body, the unfortunate husband wound up in the hospital with seizures. For her concoctions, this Mary received a sentence of two to six years.

Rooney munched another slider.

Typhoid Mary, he learned by reading another clipping, was less overtly malicious but far more deadly. Her name was Mary Mallon. Between 1901 and 1907, she had cooked for several wealthy New York families. Unknowingly, she carried the dreadful typhoid organism, *Salmonella typhosa*. A person could be a carrier of the dreaded microbe for years and never contract typhoid. Through Mary Mallon's contaminated handling of food, she had spread the disease to countless others.

Jim broke a slider in half and ate only one part, hesitated a second, then gulped down the other.

In 1907 authorities caught up with Typhoid Mary and she was placed under strict supervision for three years. Mary was permitted more freedom after signing a pledge to be careful of her personal hygiene, to seek another type of employment and to report to health authorities every three months. But Typhoid Mary did not keep her promises and authorities arrested her in 1915. By then she had caused an estimated 200 cases of typhoid, with three deaths. She was institutionalized until her death in 1938.

"Poor Resurrection Mary," Jim said to himself. "How did you ever get stuck in an envelope with those two?"

Before handling the clips on Resurrection Mary, he

wiped his fingers on a napkin. He held a slider gingerly as he munched it. Something seemed to be happening. Mary was becoming, in a kidding way, personal and real to him. He remembered Paul's cryptic note, "Jim, this is for you when you clean out my desk."

Three of the stories in the clippings were written in a flip way, the Halloween-round-up type pieces that called Resurrection Mary the "hitch-hiker" ghost. Another started, "Anyone seen Mary?" He thought of the stories and of Resurrection Cemetery where he had relatives buried. He knew kids went there and looked for Resurrection Mary's grave, especially on Halloween. By writing about her again, he realized that he might arouse that same kind of curiosity.

Yet, to ignore the fact that, in people's minds, Resurrection Mary existed was no answer. Whether the investigator was a teenager who kept one eye open while passing the cemetery or a reporter, Resurrection Mary was a phenomenon to be explored.

The story he next selected to read was the one his friend Paul Kowalski had written:

Unquestionably the best known ghost of Chicago is a young woman called Resurrection Mary.

Supposedly Mary was a teenager of Polish ancestry who lived 50 or 75 years ago. The story is told that she died in an accident on the way home from a dance. She was buried in Resurrection Cemetery.

Resurrection Mary is more than just the subject of a ghost story. She is a bond among people on the Southwest Side of the city. She is a minor cult, a shared belief and an initiation rite for teenagers. When you learn to drive and a car becomes available, you test the reality of the myth. You drive along Archer Avenue and look for her. If you are brave, you might do it alone, but preferably a friend or two go along. It is a ceremony and it isn't important if you don't actually encounter her. Seeing a young woman in the distance who might be Resurrection Mary can be quite enough.

Still, there are individuals who say they have met and been chilled by the eerie presence of the girl who lived years ago. It might be a close relative, but more often it's someone your father works with or a friend of an aunt. That it is an older person, not someone in the same age group, lends considerable credence to the story.

Though similar, each version has a distinctive mark. It usually goes like this: At a dance in the old neighborhood, two boys meet a young blonde girl. She is an excellent but aloof dancer. She asks for a ride home. She begs them to stop at the gates of Resurrection Cemetery. She goes in and disappears. She has given them her address. It is in the Back of the Yards neighborhood. Worried, they go to the house the next day. An older woman answers the door. She tells them she once had a daughter with the name they give, but that the girl died 10 years earlier. The daughter, she says, loved to dance but had been killed in a carriage accident. She is now buried in Resurrection Cemetery. The boys start to go away. The woman calls them back, shows them a photograph. It is a picture of the same young girl they had left at the cemetery the night before.

These young men, the teller assures you, were known by many people, and stuck by their story for years after their adolescence. Other versions of the same story are told, but always with the details of the dance and the mother with the picture. Sometimes Mary was hitchhiking a ride to Resurrection Cemetery or just jumped into a passing car. It is said her handprints were burned into the iron bars on the fence surrounding the cemetery and could be seen there for a dozen years or more.

On the Southwest Side of Chicago, they will swear to you the stories are true and they happened just that way. They tell you Resurrection Mary really exists. They'll bet their souls on it.

Why do people believe in her? Because the story about her is too detailed and too interesting to be a complete falsehood. And life, without such mysteries, is boring.

The article reminded Jim of Paul. He knew that when Paul had written it in 1967, he had been ill and coming into work only periodically.

"So, Paul," he mumbled, looking at the file, "this is the Resurrection Mary whom you want me to check out."

Jim's comment had been loud enough to be overheard by a young girl standing near his table. She looked maybe 18 years old. Powder on her nose and cheeks attempted to cover some pimples. Her hair arched high in a bouffant beehive that seemed to be a foot above her head. Her mouth played with a tiny, timid smile. Her eyes seemed large, a glowing green that reminded Jim of the forest girl in *Green Mansions.*, albeit a Chicago version.

"You're trying to find Resurrection Mary?" she asked shyly.

"I am" Jim answered, confused by her intrusion. "How'd you know?"

"I heard you and saw that envelope you were reading," she said. "About Resurrection Mary. It made me real curious."

"You know about her?"

"Sure, everybody does."

"You haven't run into her, have you?" he asked with a laugh.

"Nope, I haven't," Janice O'Leary said. There were several seconds of awkward silence.

"You know," she said, "I had a very strange thing happen tonight. There was this bad car accident. My boyfriend, he had an argument with a cop. Then I heard music in the woods. Hey, I might have seen her hearse tonight."

"Wait a minute. Slow down, young lady. What are you talking about? A car accident, a hearse, music in the woods?"

He realized that he had probably run into one of the teenagers he had set out to find for the newspaper.

"Where's your boyfriend?"

She was alone. Eddie had driven back to the accident scene. She had been too scared to go back or to go home as had her friend, Nancy. Eddie simply had left her at the White Castle, announcing he would come back for her later. Jim wanted to offer Janice a slider, except he realized he had already eaten them all.

"Tell me about the music. Wait a minute. I'm a newspaper reporter and my name is Jim Rooney. I figure it's only fair to inform people of that before I start getting what might be quotes."

"So?"

"Be careful about anything you ever tell a reporter."

"Like what?"

"Like, if you kids were drag-racing."

"We weren't. Junior and Eddie just wanted to prove I hadn't seen Resurrection Mary's hearse."

"And it was a car accident and a boy was killed. Did you know him?"

"No."

"What about the music?"

"It was like the trees were singing at his funeral."

"You have a vivid imagination."

"Maybe it wasn't my imagination."

"You're sure you weren't drag-racing?"

"No, actually, like we were, well, you know, making out. But please, please, don't tell anybody. If it got back to Eddie ... Please don't tell anybody. You don't know Eddie."

"Only Busby," he promised her, laughing. "I will tell only Busby."

CHAPTER FOUR
ℰℛ

7 p.m. Monday, September 9, 1968

Ed Wolinski and his son Eddie had gone at it, bull versus bulldog. Thinking he had the better of his muscle-ripping, snorting father, Eddie opened the door and left the house. "It's gonna work," Ed congratulated himself. "Reverse psychology. The little bastard."

Ed stood in front of the hallway mirror. His eyes paid little attention to his crewcut and leathery face. Instead they riveted on the size and proportion of his upper torso. His shoulders were enormous. He tensed his muscles. Twenty-five years ago, when he had been 16, he had worked hard at body building, first with a course he sent away for so he would not be a 98-pound weakling and later with weights and sophisticated equipment in the training gym at the Police Academy.

In the mirrored reflection Ed managed to ignore his paunch, the result of a wife who liked to cook and his own fondness for two six packs of Meister Brau daily.

In a day when Polish cops were not an accepted part of the predominantly Irish force, Ed's grandfather had survived and made sergeant. He had to be a little better, stronger and smarter to make it. Two of his sons had also been on the force. Ed's father had made detective.

Aside from a shoot-out in which he had captured a gas station hold-up man, Ed's greatest accomplishment was that he had escaped from Chicago. He lived in Lyons, an older suburb southwest of the city. He kept his legal address at his mother's, however, because police regulations required, and

Mayor Daley insisted, that city employees live within Chicago's boundaries

This was the door that Jim Rooney would have knocked on. The Green Dodge, license number 342-789, was registered to Ed's wife. Although they had encountered each other once before, Jim would not have recognized Ed. In Lincoln Park two weeks earlier during the Democratic convention, Ed, his nameplate in his pocket and billyclub drawn, had come at Jim from behind.

Life held a big disappointment for Ed Wolinski, but there was no one he could tell this to except Sarah, his current girlfriend. He felt full responsibility that his son would become a Chicago cop, as he and his father and grandfather had before him. At first Eddie had done so well in school that his father feared he might get too smart and think being a cop was beneath him. In the end, Eddie dropped out. He was flunking anyway. Even then he brought home impressive authors from the world of literature to flaunt at his father. He paged through Rabelais, Milton and Yeats—while getting an "F" in literature. By this time Ed spoke to his son only through "Mother" and, even then, very little.

Two things helped Ed forget his disappointment. One was women. Lately it had been Sarah. She was an attractive 38-year-old, red-haired bartender who was sharp and seemed to like telling him what a nice body he had.

Second, and more important to Ed, was his seniority. He had been on the street for over 20 years. When he and a partner broke down a door, he went in first. Of everything in his life, this probably meant the most. It was an adrenalin thing, and more than prestige. He was on the point. He took the chances. He held the dice. He lived to knock down that door.

Ed did not know what had happened to Eddie, but he did know when his son changed. Eddie had been 12. One day he had gone to school and when he came home that night, things were different.

What had happened was that Pam Pildudski, an embittered ex-girlfriend of Ed's, decided to get back at him through his son. She taught in Eddie's school. She invited Eddie, a seventh grader at the time, out for a Coke.

"I'm worried about your father," she said. "I am afraid of what might happen to him."

She explained that his father was a nice man and that they had had a relationship, but Ed was right to cut it off. She was worried that he was going to get caught taking a bribe. "Could you help?"

Eddie's belief and boasts to his friends about his father had been supported by Ed's repeated assurances that others might be on the take but he was not. Eddie cursed at Miss Pildudski for lying.

"I understand," she said, but nevertheless his father was in trouble and she was worried. She also said she could prove it. Eddie said that his father never ever had lied to him.

Miss Pildudski snuck Eddie into a bar on his father's beat. They waited, hidden in a booth. Promptly at 5 o'clock, Ed showed up to collect "for the station." Even then, Eddie wanted to think it was for the policeman's fund or something. But his father did not like the very vocal older woman who owned the bar. They got into an argument about the payoff going up the next week. Ed enumerated the violations he "forgot," such as drink-watering, bookmaking, and occasional prostitution. He hinted that drugs were sold.

Eddie spat at Miss Pildudski, but he waited until his father was long gone before leaving. From that day on, even his mother never saw any softness in him. She always had known his father lied to him, Eddie decided. She was part of the deception. Now he had but one goal, to be the opposite of the fawning, friendly, ready-to-please child in orbit around his father. Ed might have admired Eddie's new single-mindedness and vicious attitude toward the world, except that it interfered with his own plans for his Eddie to be a cop. Eddie's grades slid, and he dropped out of high school in his junior year. No way was he ever going to the Police Academy

A plot for Ed to get Eddie back on course started with one of those very rare intimate conversions between Ed and his wife. "Mother", as he called her, had not let her unfaithful husband or unhappy son know how much she cried over them. Somehow, finally, she decided she had to intervene in Eddie's life. She sat on a high-back oak chair in the parlor of the rectory. Her eyes did not look up at the cassocked man of 40 sitting behind a desk.

"Eddie needs to be something," she said to the assistant pastor. "He needs to be happy. I think he knows about his father. That is why I think he has to be a sourpuss and to act angry at everybody. I tell him all the time, 'Eddie, you get married. You got a nice girl. You marry her. Maybe you have children?' I think he's a good boy and children will make him a good man. But it's like if I say it, he not want to do it."

"Your husband, Ed, is a fine man," the priest said. "He does a lot of favors for us here at the rectory. The boy will listen to him, Mrs. Wolinski. Talk to your husband about it. Encourage them to talk. If the boy has something bothering him, and it's probably just a little thing, it'll come out. It'll be good for them to talk."

When his wife hesitatingly approached Ed with this advice, he was confused. Ed did not think that such a conversation would be an easy thing with Eddie. God knows, he told himself, he had tried his best good-guy/bad-guy tactics on him. Ed told his girlfriend, Sarah, about the situation because he needed someone to come up with an answer.

"So what can I do?" he asked.

When he had to make a decision, he always liked to throw the ball to someone else. He saw himself as a man of action. He hated to plan, but quickly criticized those who did when things got fouled up. Sarah was a planner, one of many things he had failed to acknowledge in the 18 months of their on-and-off relationship.

"I got an idea," she offered. "This kid would not do a thing you suggested for all the tea in China, right?"

"Damned right!"

"You want him to get married, right?"

"Yeah."

"Then tell him you don't want him to get married. Tell him you don't like his girlfriend and offer him a car if he doesn't marry her."

"Sarah, that's it," he said, "I'll be glad I thought of that."

Ed carried out the plan. Eddie, taking the bait, cursed his father. After slamming the door on the way out of the house, he went to see Janice O'Leary to tell her she was going to marry him.

"I'll show my stupid-ass father where he can put that car," Eddie bragged to Junior.

Half an hour later

Riccardo's Restaurant was a place where Chicago's newspapermen ate lunch and supper and swished their griefs, real or imagined, in various alcoholic beverages. Just north of the river, it stood half-way between the Michigan Avenue home of the *Tribune* and *Chicago's American* and the Wabash Avenue building of the *Sun Times* and *Daily News*.

Above the restaurant and bar on the second floor, a group of buzzing, agitated newspaper, radio and TV reporters filled a room, sitting or standing against the walls.

"We stand here tonight at a watershed in journalism," Arthur Vasser, a tall, burly expatriate reporter from the East Coast, lectured his audience.

Jim Rooney had just walked into the room where the meeting of disgruntled reporters was being held. He was late; he was using his half-hour supper break to attend this protest gathering of Chicago's working press.

"If there's any free food, bring some back for me," Busby had said.

"Damn it," Jim said, as he saw who was speaking, "All I've got is a half hour and I'm going to have to listen to Vasser."

"A watershed," the speaker repeated dramatically, pointing his finger toward the ceiling. "Let us, therefore, be careful about whatever we say and decide here tonight." He paused.

"Bullshit!" Jim muttered. It was the kind of meeting in which one does not suggest hesitation or inaction. Those waiting to talk were like hawks circling high above a field mouse.

"Only Arthur Vasser can get away with his damned comments," Jim said to the man standing next to him. "Why? Because everybody tries to figure out what Vasser has just said or what route of logic he has just used."

"Quiet." The man hushed Jim.

Jim had wanted to pull together the loose ends left in his life from the beating in Lincoln Park. He did not want pontification from people like Vasser.

The pause was not long. The speaker was back, rolling into his subject: "So I told the managing editor. I said, 'Ted, we've got to clear the air about what the police did. We've got to focus on the real issues. Not all of us know what they are, I'll tell you."

"I do," Jim thought to himself. "Some of the people in this room got hit over the head with police billyclubs because they were doing their jobs. Damn it, why can't I just speak out and say that?"

Jim had talked at reporters' meetings before, especially union meetings. He had sounded, he felt, like a parrot repeating over and over that the union leaders did not try hard enough to get reference room people and secretaries better pay raises. But his words always seemed to be muted by a cage cover he could not see.

"Why," Jim asked himself, "can this jerk Vasser turn people on and off? Everybody agrees that he says nothing. They laugh about it. And yet an hour from now, someone will stand up to rebut some point Arthur Vasser made, some bait he left out there on a hook."

Perhaps the answer was booze. Such meetings always were held after the bar had opened. The alcohol quickly knocked the inhibitions out of people's brains. He, on the other hand, working nights, came straight from the city room, from writing an obituary or putting a second-day lead on a story.

"Yet, some of these people are as sober as I am," Jim thought.

Jim saw other reporters in the room. Chris Chandler and

Brian Boyer of the *Sun-Times,* the rare kind of reporters willing to ask as tough questions of their employers as of someone they were sent to interview. Hank DeZutter and Norman Mark of the *Daily News,* who had a sense of what independence should mean for journalists. Ron Dorfman was there, a bright young guy who was education editor at the *American.*

Others were there, many whose faces he barely knew. Abe Peck and Flora Johnson from the underground paper, *The Seed,* were next to Bob Cross, a reporter from the *Tribune.*

Paul belonged here. Paul, who was in the ground, dead and buried, should have been here to raise his hand, tell his anecdotes, and share his convictions. The real leaders here were a small group of Paul's type of people. They were the believers like Chandler, Boyer, Cross and Dorfman. As angry as Jim was, it seemed they were angrier.

"Jim, you missed Betty Washington from the *Defender,*" a reporter from the *Daily News* whispered.

"What did she say?" Jim asked, not caring that he and some others across the long room were talking loudly enough to draw attention away from Arthur Vasser.

"She said the white reporters have finally experienced police brutality in Chicago. Negroes had been yelling about it for years, but the news media paid no attention, always taking a cop's word against a Negro's."

"She's got a point," Jim said.

"She wasn't, I think, very sympathetic toward the reporters who got hit," the man said, apologetically to Jim. "People like you."

Jim passed it off. He wasn't looking for sympathy.

Just then the booming voice of a gruff, ancient rewrite man from a wire service stopped all other sounds in the room: "I'm going to say something, and say it now, even if it means interrupting Mr. Vasser here."

There was applause. The room came to attention as he continued: "My mother used to have a standing question about her kids' bellyaching. 'So, what you gonna do about it?' she'd ask. God, it was a tough question. It is the only one we face tonight. I don't care about watersheds. I don't care if all of us don't agree perfectly. We have been physically and professionally attacked. Let's organize. We need a working press association just like some people have already suggested here tonight. We need a statement sent to our bosses, an idea that has also been proposed here tonight. And we need a group to get together to publish a journalism review, like some people want. We got to do all those things. We got to do something."

Jim could not see the man's face. He knew the voice well, however.

"Why couldn't I have said a third of that! Or anything? At least, they're going to move toward action," Jim thought.

Just then another speaker interrupted, "I've got four points I'd like to make in response to Mr. Vasser's comments."

Jim Rooney wanted to yell, and at least four others, guffawed. He looked at his watch. He had to get back. He would get a report the next day. This time he really wanted to stay angry. Jim thought of Arthur Vasser. He looked around the room to see what Vasser's reaction might be to the speaker. Vassar had left for the bar on the first floor.

There was no free food. It was not a freebie. He did not have to take back a doggie bag for Busby. That at least brought a passing smile.

❦

CHAPTER FIVE

 ∽

A Loop bookstore

4:30 P.M., Wednesday

"Theodore's Used Book Emporium," read the gold-leaf letters on the window. The small store had been on Wells Street in the Loop for 47 years. It looked remarkably like a well-tended private library of rare books.

Theodore Wozik, a white-haired man of 80 with a ski-slope mustache, peeked out at the world over oblong, bifocal glasses.

Often in the evenings before going to work, Jim dropped in at the store for an hour or two. The owner slumped in a soft old chair behind the counter, usually had his face in the current issue of *American Bookman's Weekly* or some catalogue of books for sale. He greeted Jim, calling him "James," without looking up.

"People treating you all right?" Jim asked.

"People are all right," Theodore countered.

"Hah!" Jim challenged. "Anyone one who has come into this store in the last 50 years knows that you like good books better than you do people."

"What does that mean?"

"About books, you say 'Condition, condition, condition.' You would scream bloody murder if a customer came in here and wanted to sell you a book not in mint condition or without a dust jacket.

" 'Mint' is a word for coins, not books," Theodore said.

"And I'm talking about book jackets, not that old one you are wearing, Theodore. You don't care how you look, but you do care about the look of your books. Therefore, my point is proven—you like books more than people."

"That is typical, James."

"Listen, Theodore, I have a question. Look into your crystal ball. I am looking for Resurrection Mary—you know, the ghost, or at least someone who claims he ever danced with her. I want to do a story. I would like to know what you think. Am I going to find her?"

"You are looking for a ghost, and you ask Theodore if you are going to find her?"

"Yes." Jim answered. "You have the information that has rubbed off from the ten thousand books that pass through your hands every year. I appeal to your mercenary soul. Sell me a book that has the answer in it."

"I find no hard evidence in any book to establish that there are ghosts," Theodore said with the deliberateness of a scholastic philosopher.

"Then you are saying, Theodore, that I won't find Resurrection Mary or any trace of her?"

"No. I'm not saying that. Let me tell you something. In my younger days, both Harry Houdini and Clarence Darrow were customers who came into my shop. They were the world's two greatest skeptics. Yet, each one said that, if there were any possible way, he would come back after he died."

"And to the enormous disappointment of their followers, neither one did." Jim challenged his friend, "You say you knew them both?"

"That's why one has a bookstore, James. Eventually everyone who is a serious thinker will come into it. Darrow and Houdini both, if you'll pardon the expression, haunted bookstores. Let me tell you a story about each of them."

"Have I ever refused such a request?"

"Of course not. You're not permitted to. Of the two of us, one owns this establishment, and it isn't you, James."

"*Capish.*"

"Don't try Italian on me. I'm Polish."

"Get on with the stories."

"Darrow, first. See this book. It was once in his library. There's his bookplate. Clarence loved books and he accumulated quite a few. People were always sending him their latest attempts at literary immortality."

"Didn't he also write a novel?" Jim asked.

"Yes, a couple, actually, *Farmington* and *An Eye for an Eye*. But what I want to get at is what he did with his books after he died."

"He came back after he died and did something?"

"Stop trying to ruin a good story, James. In his will, Clarence Darrow left a provision that his books should be distributed to as many people as possible. This was around 1938. The executors of his estate held a big sale. You could pick up a rare, signed first edition for 25 cents, one that Clarence Darrow had owned."

"That could have knocked the bottom out of the book market in Chicago."

"No. It did just the opposite. It hooked people. It helped make some people life-long book addicts, people striving for a better life. The year 1938 was during the Depression. In hopeless times, people seek solace in books."

"And what about Houdini?"

"That story involves the Chicago newspapers. You're not the first representative of a paper to go ghost-hunting. Do you know the guy who is head of the *American*'s photo studio?"

"Tony Berardi, Sr. Great guy. When he was younger, I think he was a boxer."

"He's the one who I think was involved. Back in the '20s, spiritualists and seances were big, real big. There was one who was especially good at summoning up spirits. I still remember her name, Mrs. Minnie Reichert. Now, Minnie could conduct a seance and you wouldn't know where all those voices were coming from. She claimed she didn't use a long trumpet or any other device to project her voice in the darkened basement where she held the seance. Houdini had Berardi and some other guy sneak a camera in a doctor's bag into her basement."

"Who told you all this?"

"Harry Houdini, later, when he came around looking for obscure magic books. It was also in the paper the next day. Photographers in those days had to explode phosphorous to take pictures in the dark. Berardi flashed his and turned the darkened basement into day when he snapped Minnie's picture.

"Let me guess what the woman had in her hand. Was it the trumpet that she claimed she didn't use?"

"Exactly. It was about six feet long. She looked as though she had been given the job of raising the dead with it. Now, according to Houdini, there was nobody in the world who could get angrier than a psychic who had just been exposed. He should have known because he had done it hundreds of times. The way I heard it, those guys he sent had to scramble through a basement window to get out alive."

"That sounds real discouraging for my search for Resurrection Mary. Do you think that I might find fraud?"

"No, but I would say there is plenty of reason to be discouraged. Stories of reappearing young girl ghosts are told in different variations in every major city in this country and in other cultures as well. Often it is a girl hitch-hiking by a cemetery. Some versions I've read date the story back to before the turn of the century in New England. They're all based on hearsay."

"Then, I am on a silly, wild ghost chase? I think that's what I really know anyway."

"Maybe not, Jim." Theodore had never called him "Jim" before.

"Why not?"

"Go on your search. Would I have told Don Quixote to stay home, or Columbus or Ponce de Leon not to go on their impossible quests?"

"You're trying to be overdramatic, Theodore."

"Perhaps, but there is drama in what you are doing. You are going into a magical place, the world of myths. You know I like stories. These books around me are stories. And that is what you are in search of: not facts, not a person, but a story."

"I understand," Jim said. "You want me to come back and tell you about it so you can harangue other customers with the story of your friend, the reporter, searching for Resurrection Mary."

"Precisely. I also happen to think that there is a remote possibility you are going to find something. You may not find the exact story you are looking for, but you can still stumble across a good story. You've got that ability. Some people would say, 'This is not what I am looking for, so, I give up'."

"You think I'll find something then?"

"I don't know. I am from the Back of the Yards neighborhood. When I was very young I learned about this story. I overheard some older people talking in Polish about it. I didn't understand too well. I remember I had a dream about her. It's just that a story was told. Somehow it seemed to be in a different form than what you hear today."

"Was it about Resurrection Mary, Theodore?"

"There were two words from it that I can recall for certain. Only two."

"What are they?"

"Two names."

"Was one 'Mary', Theodore?"

"Yes, it was the Polish version of 'Mary'."

"And the other?"

"A nickname. It seems as though it were 'Bud'. That was a long time ago. I just can't be sure."

"Any more details? Any sense of what the story was about? Why do you identify it with Resurrection Mary?"

"Maybe I shouldn't have brought it up. That conversation from my childhood always comes to my mind when anyone mentions Resurrection Mary. Like when you first meet someone and it is so ... it stays with you. I've always felt that was when I first learned of her. But the details are just not there."

"Do you have any leads? Any ancient relatives I can talk to? Who were the people you heard talking about her?"

"I don't recall, James. I'm sorry. I have no leads at all. But maybe you'll find one. Perhaps Mary and her story are out there waiting for you."

"What do you mean?"

"It's a feeling."

"Who are you, Theodore? A well-read bookseller and friend of Chicago's literati, or a Pole from the Back of the Yards who still believes in ghosts?"

"I am both, James. Who are you? You don't believe in ghosts. So what are you going to do if you find one."

"I won't find a ghost, Theodore."

"Mary ... Bud," the bookowner murmured, trying to stir an almost 80-year-old memory.

The newspaper office

10 P.M., Wednesday

Jim Rooney had had his conference with the managing editor. It was a disappointment, although not entirely. Jim believed the key to suggesting any idea to people in the front office was simple—make them think it is their idea.

He started by reminding his managing editor of their conversation a year earlier when the editor of the paper had complimented a piece Jim had written about the Southwest Side.

"Whadyathink?" Jim asked. "Should we combine the ideas? Make a regular column out of neighborhood stories? This newspaper's ready for something new."

Jim knew the higher echelons of the paper were considering a new format and were searching for ideas.

"Write me a memo," his boss replied. "Lay out a little more of the history of one area. I see it more as a series than a column."

This was not what Jim had hoped for. A limited series was not the escape plan that had started to well in his chest. "Resurrection Mary" he scratched on a piece of paper, then added, "off nights" and "column." He pressed his pen, making a heavy check mark after each item on his list.

"You're going to quit being a loser," a voice within him chided. "Write the memo."

Jim wrote it, but held back his trump card, Resurrection Mary. The managing editor, in the mood he was in, might see Mary as a good idea and suggest a one-shot piece. Jim knew he had to focus on neighborhoods. He would give the Southwest Side some historical perspective in what he sent to the front office. From the research he himself would learn as much as he could about the area and any roots a ghostly legend might have there.

3 P.M., Thursday

In the newspaper's reference library Jim found eight shelves of books on Chicago history. He opened a large, leather-bound one, written in 1884 by A. T. Andreas and titled *History of Cook County*. The second half was about those areas, such as Hyde Park and Lake View, which were "suburbs" then. In 1884, the Southwest Side had been a rural marsh.

Further research among the books on the shelves had indicated the history of the Southwest Side had never really been written. Much of the memo would have to be drawn directly from his own knowledge and experiences.

Jim typed:

Memo to managing editor from Jim Rooney For neighborhood articles on Chicago's Southwest Side, Sept. 12, 1968.

If you head out Archer Avenue, you traverse Chicago's Southwest Side, where second and third generation Europeans have created a compromise between the Old World and the new. The single family homes, brick bungalows and box-like single story structures comprise a hodge-podge built after World

War II. They were constructed for young families fleeing "old neighborhoods" such as Bridgeport, McKinley Park, the Back of the Yards, or Brighton Park. Older, larger wooden houses here and there are remnants of the area's rural past.

There is more lore than history. Tales are told and the knowledge of them binds the people. Often they involve a bizarre or a grizzly murder such as that of the Grimes sisters. Missing for months, the frozen bodies of the young women were found near a culvert on Old German Church Road. Over a decade later people still know the details and can point out the culvert.

Sometimes the story or rumor is fresh or supposedly so. In one frequently repeated account, a young boy is sent into the washroom of a local store or a roller rink by his mother. The child screams. Mom rushes in. Her son has been castrated. The man who did it left through a window or the transom. In each retelling, the story is substantiated by the fact that the boy's father or uncle is related to someone who knew or worked with the person telling the story. The credibility of the tale rests not on facts but on the structure of familiar places and the names of people who know people.

A girl's school has a nun who haunts it. Sister So and So was raising funds for the new auditorium, and the very day it was to be dedicated, she was killed in a car accident on Archer Avenue. This nun now is seen often in the auditorium, especially on occasions such as graduation or the anniversary of her death. It is said that on the last day of a girl's attendance at the school, she has the greatest chance of seeing the nun.

These tales, these legends, together weave into a tapestry that presents a neighborhood of people caught between the science of today and the mythology of the past.

The Southwest Side does have a history, a strange one.

In the days of the Lake Michigan outpost known first as Fort Dearborn, what is today known as the Southwest Side of Chicago was then called Mud Lake.

The civilized and uncivilized world had many mud lakes in the early 19th Century, but none so important as this one. It was a major world highway, the passage way to the Mississippi River and its rich valley.

Indians, French explorers and fur trappers, and American pioneers all had a need for a navigable passage between the Great Lakes and the Mississippi River. They found it at Chicago. Only a few miles separated the Chicago and Des Plaines Rivers, which led in turn to the Illinois and then to the Mississippi rivers. The short area between the Chicago and the Des Plaines Rivers was Mud Lake.

"If any ghost were hanging around the Southwest Side," Jim thought, "its soul must have been cursed with the vile, rancorous epithets uttered by French fur traders who pushed through leeches, mosquitoes, and mud." Jim easily could imagine those French voyagers cursing every inch of that mud as they pushed their bodies through Mud Lake. The heavens must have resounded with their "Mon Dieu's" and their swearing.

જ

CHAPTER SIX

ᗢ

Early afternoon, Monday

The young woman in front of Jim—he didn't know who she was or why she was there—was naked. She was fifteen or sixteen, little more than a child. There was a puffiness to her face, which seemed unusually pale. Her hair, long and blonde, fell over her shoulders. He had been talking to a different person, an older woman, and suddenly this young girl was there.

He once had covered the murder of a prostitute who was even younger. Jim had experienced the same painful sense of grief that he did now and a bizarre curiosity kept him focused on questioning who she was and what was it she wanted.

The girl stroked her long hair as though awkwardly trying to lure him, yet appearing lost in a dreamlike confusion.

They were alone, the two of them. Who was she? What should he do? He wanted to cover her, but he had nothing with which to do it. Something was wrong; something, very confused. He sensed he had the power to leave and used that escape.

It was one o'clock in the afternoon, two hours before he usually awoke up for work.

The girl in the dream remained vividly with him.

Was this some subconscious image of Resurrection Mary? The question repeated itself with an obsessive urgency. He shook himself more fully awake and pulled his half-awake body out of bed.

"There was something, no there were several things

wrong with that dream," he reasoned as he tried to collect his thoughts.

"Resurrection Mary is supposed to be more beautiful than this girl, more aloof and definitely more elegant. Hey, where was the white flowing gown they mention in all the stories about her? This girl lacked any kind of a romantic aura and that has been essential to the Resurrection Mary legend."

Maybe, if he would divert his attention by shaving, he thought, his mind would let the subject go. But as he lathered his face, he was not even aware of his motions. He focused on the dream. It had to be, he assured himself, some kind of a subconscious expression of the ghost story with whom he was becoming involved so intensely. But why was the dream image so different from the legend?

Jim went to the window of his seventh floor kitchenette apartment on Sheridan Road. He looked out over Lake Michigan and saw a flock of geese flying south along the warm flyway near the shore. No matter how many times he saw them in formation, it still pleased him. For a couple of seconds Jim forgot both his dream and Resurrection Mary, concentrating on the scene before him.

Then, snapping his fingers quickly as he remembered something, he turned and reached for his reporter's notebook. Leafing through its pages, he located the paragraph for which he was searching.

Jim smiled as he read.

Until now he had no doubt in his mind about what Resurrection Mary was supposed to look like. Riding a bus several days earlier he had written a paragraph, a fantasized description of her for any future story he might compose. He re-read it:

> You noticed first the faraway mystical look in Mary's sad eyes. She was a slender, graceful young woman of 17 with a face you could imagine holding a smile but which didn't. Her hair was silken, a bright gold yellow. Mary's dress was white and

flowed in the wind along with her hair. She was beautiful and graceful beyond her tender years.

Except for the blonde hair, there was no similarity with the image of the girl his sleep had conjured up. He suddenly realized he was a little frightened by something, but he didn't know what. Until now Mary never could have scared him. Her story had chilled others, but not him. No goose pimples. The reason was simple. The Mary with whom he had been dealing was a projection he could change at will. If he made her incredibly beautiful, he did so to tell a better story, a more frightening one. When he wanted to re-create her through writing about her, he merely had to make certain that her image agreed with what people expected to read.

The phone rang, and its sound unnerved him. He caught his breath and tried to regain his composure before answering.

"Daddy—Mommy said I got to ask you if it's all right ..."

Jim sighed.

"If only she'd ask me how I am?" He wished he had enough faith in his relationship with his nine-year-old daughter, Judy, to tell her his thoughts.

"Can I?" she asked. He realized he had missed the question.

"Can you what, honey?"

"Oh Daddy," the little girl said impatiently, "Can I not come this weekend so I can sleep over at Jennie's?"

To say "yes" to her meant "no" for his plans to be with her, but, of course, he said "yes" to his daughter.

Thanking him sweetly, she abruptly hung up.

Why didn't he just go away on a trip and forget all his problems, he wondered. Her phone call had ended the immediacy of his dream, but he returned to it now as a distraction, searching for new details. The girl's face and her body had been puffy. There had been another woman. He could not remember a thing about her. Maybe it was the girl's mother. He just did not know.

What else? Something else seemed important. The girl

had been aware of his presence. Even though she stared blankly, she seemed to know he was there. He was certain. She awkwardly tried to entice him, to lure him.

What was all this nonsense? He really did not believe in Resurrection Mary. Was he getting into this on some strange, upsetting emotional level? Maybe he was getting too intense. Perhaps, before he proceeded, he should remind himself again that he did not believe that Resurrection Mary ever existed.

"Actually, I couldn't believe in a ghost even if I wanted to."

Then Jim remembered about his daughter. He would not see her this weekend. His ex-wife probably had engineered the sleep-over. At the moment, unlike Resurrection Mary, Judy was painfully real to him. Jim picked up the phone. He was going to call back.

For once, he was going to assert himself to her. He started to dial the number he once had shared with his wife and daughter. At the next to last number he stopped. Why put himself through the pain? He slammed down the phone. He hurt, but he could not find his way through the suffering to touch within himself what he really desired—a little girl he wanted to be with. He thought of the charges that his wife, in her anger and frustration, had thrown at him during the divorce. She had been brutally honest for the first time. She had called him "emotionally frozen." Would honesty have saved their relationship? Not until they were mired in their arguments and fighting did he begin to have a glimmer of what the truth was, what his limits were.

"You intellectualize your relationships," she told him. "And I'm angry because you've done it to us."

Now, Jim thought, he needed a distraction such as Resurrection Mary to forget what he really wanted but couldn't obtain.

"Judy, my little girl, I never intellectualized her," he said defiantly.

Tuesday, 7 P.M.

"You're not going to do it," Eddie said, a statement and a command.

Janice, for the first time, had a cause she felt as strongly about as Eddie did. Looking down to the side, she shrugged her shoulders ever so slightly.

Eddie glared at her, his silence finally broken with "You're not."

Even more than Janice, Junior knew that Eddie would take action to back up his edict. When Eddie had announced to Janice that he was going to marry her, it was clear that she did not question it. Now he was telling her she couldn't pursue the search for Resurrection Mary with the newspaper reporter.

Janice knew, come what may, that for the first time she would not obey Eddie.

Eddie realized that what she attempted to do would take her away from his control. He understood power the way a Chicago politician does. He knew about the Democratic machine, and how it worked at the precinct level, which was where it counted.

"The political machine's gut response," Eddie once told Junior, "is to want everything and anything more than the other guy. That is power."

Eddie despised Republicans, not because of their platform or personalities, but because they did not want votes in Cook County strongly enough to out-connive the Democrats. He felt the same way about the decisions other kids made. He wanted things more vehemently than others did; therefore, he should have them. This determination especially endeared him to Junior, who worshipped someone who could bring excitement into his life while making all the major decisions that Junior couldn't and didn't want to make. Now Janice was challenging Eddie's authority, wanting to make an independent choice, Janice who was engaged to be Eddie's wife.

Later, Junior and Nancy both attempted to talk her out of her decision.

"He really ain't going to like it," Nancy said. "I mean you're really not going to do it, are you? I mean, I can't even imagine you trying. I mean, he's gonna yell at you for even thinking about it. Maybe you could apologize and he'll forget you thought about it. I mean, geeze, I would."

"He'll stop you," Junior said. He did not feel he had to say more.

"Will you help me?" Janice asked Junior.

"No."

She appreciated the short answer. At least it might mean that Junior would not report this conversation to Eddie. That was all she could ask or expect. Meanwhile, she would chart her own course and take the consequences.

A home on the Southwest Side

1 A.M., Wednesday

Janice pulled down a shopping bag from a shelf in her bedroom. A frayed *Chicago Tribune* map was in the bag. References were hand-written on it about Southwest Side happenings she had heard about since she was in the seventh grade.

Next to Mount Carmel Cemetery were two names: "Al Capone" and "Julia Buccola." Holy Sepulchre Cemetery had the name "Mary Alice Quinn" written over it. The Indian grave of Alexander Robinson was marked with his Indian name, "Chinchipinquay." Indian mounds were indicated in several locations.

Also in the bag was a small container of earth taken from the grave of Mary Alice Quinn.

"Mary Alice," she said, talking to the vial. "This dirt is supposed to bring good luck. Maybe you can help us find somebody who met your friend Resurrection Mary and not let Eddie get too mad."

She looked at the map and counted the number of times she had written "Resurrection Mary" on it. There were four.

"Eddie's really gonna blow up over what I'm going to do," she said to herself and sighed. "I'll need all the help I can get." She meant it as a prayer.

လ

CHAPTER SEVEN

❧

An apartment in the Canalport neighborhood

---

8 P.M., Wednesday

"To understand Chicago," Sarah often told bar customers, "you got to come to the neighborhoods, especially the old ones, and stroll any block.

"How dirty the street are, that tells you how much clout your alderman's got. Deterioration and payoffs go hand in hand. Look for boarded-up buildings, abandoned cars, teenagers buying liquor, policy or numbers receipts on the sidewalks, prostitutes, dilapidated hotels that warehouse ex-mental patients, clinics where they buy your blood, and day labor offices. These all need police and political clout to flourish. These problems supply the fat that greases corruption."

Sarah was a walker. Up and down the streets of her neighborhood she strode.

It was Wednesday, her night off. Instead of having Ed over, she had done laundry and washed her hair. She did the two together only when she already was depressed. Then, she put on her silk, dragon-embroidered jacket and went out to the street.

Sarah's neighborhood prided itself on being the geographic center of Chicago. It was also, she believed, the forgotten, ignored middle child of the city, with its dirty streets, boarded-up buildings and lack of new businesses.

It was Sarah's turf: a funeral parlor, Our Lady of Good Counsel Church, the old religious gift shop, a yard full of a roofer's tar-stained equipment, a real estate office with curled-up property ads, a boarded-up athletic club. It was one of the city's oldest neighborhoods and its lack of change bore a reassuring familiarity for Sarah.

"Ed, that ape," she kept saying. That word she used for him had once had a special meaning to her. It had spoken of his strength and of his virile torso. Now she repeated it to remind herself of his insensitivity.

He had grown tired of Sarah, not entirely, but mostly. Her red hair, even her red hair, had begun to bore him. She denied it to herself, but she knew. Her usual request for him not to leave his coat on the floor had begun to sound to him like his wife's nagging, he said. Such comparisons marked the beginnings of the end of a relationship for him. He had told her that once and she painfully remembered it now.

What had been one of Sarah's beguiling traits, her aggressiveness, was becoming an annoyance to Ed. She recognized the signals. The hunt would soon start, probably already had, for her replacement. The new one would need to be available and willing to wait on his needs, but mainly be someone new.

Ed demanded that she please him, yet there was no way she could. Sarah had been here several times before "with other bozos." This time she was determined to save the relationship.

"The ape," she continued muttering, still reluctant to give him any responsibility for what was happening.

She wanted Ed, if, for no other reason than because she was tired of being dumped when a man tired of her. She knew from experience what was going on.

Sarah was 38 and capable of a few tricks to help her avoid the self-effacing pleadings that such situations had evoked when she was younger. When Ed sneered or tried to start an argument, she would go for a walk or to a movie. She was beginning to see a lot of movies.

She knew that such diversions were temporary solutions. Sarah was working on a grand plan that centered on taking a trip with Ed. She had visited her friend, Lois, a travel agent.

Together they had plotted possible vacations to Mexico, the Caribbean, or an island off the coast of South Carolina. None of them fit. Lois suggested Las Vegas.

"Las Vegas isn't quite it," Sarah replied, "but it's a move in the right direction."

Her goal was to get Ed away from the city, to let herself grow on him. She had no doubt of her ability to accomplish this. He was anchored to a wife whom he neither loved nor respected. The trip would loosen this chain that ultimately choked off any other attachment. Ed lived for excitement, the adrenalin release of cops and robbers, the challenge of breaking down a door or of taking a payoff and not getting caught himself. Las Vegas was far too tame for her purposes.

"You want action?" Lois asked. "I can get a trip for you guys to the Near East. What about some place like Egypt?"

"Egypt! That's it." Sarah was weighing possibilities.

"It'll be expensive," Lois warned.

"Wrong Egypt," Sarah countered, laughing.

For a portion of her childhood, she had lived in far downstate Illinois. The southernmost part of Illinois had long been known as "Little Egypt," a nickname that dated to a famine in 1830 which had reminded the starving settlers in the northern part of the state of the biblical famine that took the sons of Jacob into the land of Egypt. In that hard winter, these pioneers, like Joseph's brothers in the Old Testament, had to go south to get grain.

When Sarah was staying with Granny Sepe, she had lived in "Bloody Williamson County." Those days and Granny, now long dead, were a faded, unpleasant blur. But they contained a nugget she now could cash in.

"Williamson County, I'm talking the 1920s and 1930s, still was the wild frontier," she told Lois. "I mean, it was wild."

She was surprised at her own enthusiasm. She had once gone to the library to find out about the area because her childhood memories had always confused her. Now she felt she could use her experience and even a little of her research.

"The county had everything," she told Lois. "There was gun battles in cars, Klan killings, labor fights, massacres, wars and hangings. I mean, it was ugly and it was wild."

Much of the Williamson County's lawlessness had been triggered on June 22, 1922, by a mob of 500 people who joined in the brutal massacre of 18 strikebreakers at a coal mine in Herrin, Illinois. Sarah's relatives had been part of the mob and for years afterward egged each other on to tell bloody details of the massacre. She left the house when they started talking about it

A year later, two organizations, the Klu Klux Klan and the Knights of the Flaming Circle, battled in the streets of Herrin until troops were called in to restore order. Two years later, more blood flowed when the rival Shelton and Birger gangs fought for control of bootlegging and other rackets in the area. Guns were replaced by bombs and the Shelton gang took to using an armored truck in making attacks on enemies such as "High Pockets" McQuay and "Casey" Jones. Everyone in Williamson County, especially in Herrin, seemed connected somehow with this. Sarah still had relatives there on her father's side. Her mother, on the other hand, was from a very peaceable Polish family in Chicago.

Sarah's relatives in Williamson County afforded her just the opportunity she needed.

"Ed craves excitement," she told Lois. "I'll take that ape to Herrin. I'll show him the cemetery on School Highway where the bloodiest part of the massacre took place. I'll take him down the streets where gang wars were fought. I'll introduce him to Uncle Clete, who was part of the Birger gang. Charlie Birger was an enemy of the Shelton gang. He testified against them, I think, and was later convicted of murder himself and hung. Uncle Clete saw the hanging and knows the inside story of the gang."

It was simple. To save her relationship with Ed Wolinski, Sarah would take him to and let him be regaled by Uncle Clete. The way she figured it, the violence of Bloody Williamson County and of her uncle's stories would rub off, and Ed would identify her with that stimulating experience. She was certain the excitement of Williamson County could do her good.

"I'll train that ape," she said.

Sarah swore mildly at herself for mentioning her plans to her mother.

"Sarah," her mother said. "You go by Peoria State Hospital. You stop and visit my Uncle Bud there. I not see him for long time, and he very, very old. He likes you, and he would want to see you, I'm sure."

Uncle Bud was Sarah's great uncle. He was well over 90. He was, she remembered, an odd, old man who possessed some kind of family secret. Sarah had a good feeling about him even though she had not seen him since her wedding to her former husband, Jules, years ago. To attend, Uncle Bud had gotten out of the mental hospital on a pass.

Sarah did not want to be reminded of Jules, and that was one of the many reasons she did not want to stop in Peoria and see Uncle Bud. The principal reason was it might spoil things with Ed. It was one thing to let him know she had an uncle in Williamson County who had been a gangster, but something else entirely to display an uncle from her mother's side who had spent almost his entire life in a mental institution.

Still, Sarah would stop in Peoria. Curiosity piqued her, but even more, it had to do with her mother. Her mother seldom asked her to do anything. The two women had very different lifestyles, but her mother never crowded or tried to change her daughter. For that Sarah was grateful. She completely believed her only means of salvation was through her mother. Even as a child, Sarah remembered her mother's exhortation, *Rosnij duza,* which means, "Grow tall." Sarah, as a child, believed her mother was urging her to be a tall girl. She wanted to please her mother, so she walked straighter than any other girl in her parochial school. The nuns used to praise her for it and point out her excellent posture to the other children

But her mother still said it to her even after she had grown up. Finally, on the day she stopped by her mother's house to tell her what the doctor had said, Sarah understood her mother's words.

"No children. I can't have children." She repeated the words to her mother. It was a terrible sentence. Sarah was an only child, and this meant her mother would never be a *Busia*, grandmother. Her mother looked Sarah in the eyes and then embraced her. Finally the words came out, *Rosnij duza*.

Sarah understood what it meant: "You have a backbone. I know. I gave it to you. It will serve you well."

And, for the first time, Sarah answered, *Bog zaplac*, which meant both "Thank you" and "I love you.

Sarah had thought of this encounter many times, especially during the miserable divorce, the factory job and then six months of unemployment. Her mother remained her support.

"I'll stop and I will see Uncle Bud," Sarah told her mother.

And she arched her back, making herself a little taller.

๛

CHAPTER EIGHT

☙

An apartment on Sheridan Road

Late Monday afternoon, September 30

Like a prisoner taking his daily exercise inside a compound, Jim paced back and forth on his carpet. Even glancing now and then out his apartment window at the lake did little to assuage his feeling that he needed to escape.

"If only they hadn't asked me," Jim groaned, banging his fist into his palm. "They" had intruded on him. They had taken the thoughts in the back of his mind, the ones he did not want to confront, and asked him to make a decision. "They" were the reporters who were pulling together the new *Chicago Journalism Review.*

A friendly afternoon phone call five days earlier had caught him off guard; he had been sleeping. One of the prospective editors of the *Review* was suggesting he write a short piece about his experiences on the street during the Democratic National Convention. The man also wanted him to comment on how the Chicago newspapers had or had not supported reporters such as himself. Jim was captured by a painful, frustrating dilemna. How could he tell the *Review* he had to buckle under to get a column? He could not explain the paper was going to change. If he said that, they would feel he had sold out. He shared their anger and believed in what they were doing and very much wanted to be a part of it.

On the other hand, Jim knew the most avid readers of the journalism review would be the editors of the dailies. While they would not get caught punishing those reporters who wrote for it, neither would they be willing to take a chance on a fledgling columnist who also wrote for the journalism review. He might chance it and write the *Review* article. But how open and honest could he really be? Jim had a conflict of interest. He did not want to compromise himself by either writing the piece or not writing it.

He played with the idea of giving up his ambition for a column. This was what compromised him. Give it up and he'd be free. But, he had to get off nights, and soon. The idea of making a decision had gnawed at him since the call. The pressure seemed to be getting to his stomach.

"Punt," Jim finally decided. "Start to write the article. See how it goes. Don't promise them anything. See how real it all is."

Yet, Jim did not want to do even that much. His no-win situation seemed to have a lot of personal pain attached to it. He was angry at the police who had beaten him and others as well as at the editors who had abandoned their reporters. He had to do something. But when he was offered a chance, the personal price tag seemed too great.

He felt like a five-year old making the complaint, but he said it anyway, "It ain't fair."

He tried to think it through: "How is this one going to get resolved? What will actually happen? What I'm going to do?" It was as though it were all happening to someone else.

It was at that moment that the phone rang. Janice O'Leary, on the other end of the line, blurted out her invitation.

"Mr. Rooney, I want you to come and visit Mount Carmel Cemetery with me."

"Cemeteries remind me of death," Jim Rooney said flatly, hoping that Janice would pick up on his reluctance to make the trip.

"Mount Carmel Cemetery is different, Mr. Rooney," she said. "I go there all the time."

"Why in heaven's name would someone go to a cemetery all the time?" Jim asked.

"I was thinkin'..."

"Well?"

"At least you oughta go to Mount Carmel."

"Why?"

"Cause you feel things there."

"Like what, Janice?"

"A ghost..."

"What do you mean?"

"Mr. Rooney, did you know they have a photograph of a ghost at Mount Carmel?"

"They what?"

Janice hesitated. The pause gave Jim time to experience the gulf between them. His memory tabbed back to what he knew about Mount Carmel Cemetery. There were gangsters and archbishops buried there, but he didn't know about any photo of a ghost. How could Janice answer that question? It was preposterous, but she had something in her head that she believed was true.

"A picture of a ghost?" he prodded.

"Well, yeah... It's Julia Buccola. The photo is on her tombstone."

"Janice," he said. "Mount Carmel is where my grandparents are buried. My mother used to take me there as a child. There are a lot of tombstones with photos on them, as I remember. It was an Italian custom 50 years ago. Is that what you mean?"

"But Mr. Rooney, Julia's has two photos. One is of her in her wedding dress, like a lot of tombstones of ladies buried there. The other photo is of her six years later."

"Well does that make it a picture of a ghost?"

"It does because the photo is from six years afterwards."

"Six years after what?"

"After she died."

"Janice, if that photo of your Julia Buccola exists, then I'll go with you to Mount Carmel Cemetery. I want to see it."

"Also, I'd like to take you to the place where I heard the music I told you about."

Jim begin to envision the details that would help him write his ghost story. Janice was offering him a beginning and possibly a diversionary story, if nothing materialized on Resurrection Mary.

"Good," he said.

"Mr. Rooney, I really want to find Resurrection Mary," Janice said.

That, or get a story trying, he thought to himself.

"Can I pick you up at your house at 4:30?" Jim asked.

"Mr. Rooney, could you please make it a half hour earlier? Eddie gets off about that time and I gotta miss him. He usually drives out to the canal with Junior, but I don't wanna be here if he comes by my house."

What had he gotten himself into, Jim wondered. Cemeteries were annoying places. He remembered the graveside services he had attended. Every one had a common denominator, a seemingly interminal wait. The delay was always for the priest or a favorite aunt to arrive. Or for the funeral director to get the rope straight. Mainly, it was for a reason he had not been informed about. Only a select few knew why whatever was supposed to be happening was not. Even as a child, he had found this true. As a reporter, he had covered several graveside services for victims of tragedies. Even then, there was the wait. Eternity passed, he once thought, while people stood or sat under a tent next to an open grave. It was as though people were not certain what they were doing. Maybe the world would come to an end or there would be some other excuse such as their waking up from a nightmare and they would not have to complete the task of burying someone they loved.

And then there was the weather at funerals and in cemeteries, which always seemed to be either inclement or else very, very good. It was never ordinary or unnoticeable. Once when he was a child and his crotchety old uncle was being buried, it had rained annoyingly. The funeral director's assistant, who was driving their car, commented, "Heaven is crying."

"Why?" Jim had asked his mother. He was finding the ready-made answers of his religion classes unsatisfying, even as a seven year old, and when someone stated God was crying over an uncle no one liked, it required an explanation.

When his mother refused to answer, Jim demanded, "I asked you why heaven would cry for old Uncle Pete anyway?"

His father, only half-concealing a smile, took his wrist and replied, "We will discuss the matter later, Jimmy."

The driver gave Jim a sharp look. In response, his father shook the man off with an impatient nod.

His parents never did pick up the discussion. In their own relationship, they were caught in a gap of faith. His mother believed in religion and his father did not. But at the time, both wanted the marriage too much to probe the question of their beliefs. They claimed they gave their son room to make his own choice, but his mother, in fact, insisted he get religious indoctrination. He learned what the nuns said. He memorized his lessons and did well on their tests. But he never believed it. To Jim Rooney, some people might believe in things they could not see, but not his father and not he.

Jim had never talked to his daughter about religion. What would he have replied if she asked him if he believed that God was crying when it rained?

"People too easily ask you to believe things that are impossible or improbable," he said to himself, fashioning a hypothetical reply.

"The idea that faith can be preposterous is too far above little Judy's comprehension. Why do I have such a need to try to pass my skepticism onto her?" he chided himself. Then his mind wandered to a thought about that funeral car driver.

Jim laughed, "Now there was an ass who really wanted you to believe!"

Late Tuesday afternoon, October 1

Across Roosevelt Road from Mount Carmel is a mammoth mausoleum, part of another Catholic cemetery, Queen of Heaven. It was meant to inspire awe both in design and size, and it does for the string of relatives who travel here to commemorate the dead. Mount Carmel, the older of the two cemeteries, has no such awesome edifice, not even a gate.

As they drove into the landscaped garden of memories and remains, Janice recited facts about the cemetery and its history. Jim, who had attended more to the rush hour traffic on Roosevelt Road than to her details, gave more heed to her words once they were inside.

The first large plot that he noticed was for a religious order, "The Sisters of Mercy of the Blessed Virgin Mary." A plaque stated that the order had been founded in 1833. That was the year that Chicago had become a village. On the grave of each nun was a tiny marker.

He noticed little photographs encased in glass on many of the older tombstones scattered throughout the cemetery, just as he had remembered them as a child. Most of the gravestones bore Italian or Irish names. Some older ones, molded in cement, had turn-of-the-century police or fire hats on them. Several had a star or badge number carved into it.

"The history of Chicago's Catholics is buried in this cemetery," he said to Janice.

Noticing a small mausoleum with the name "Genna" carved on it, Jim pulled the car off to the side of the road.

"I've got to check this out," he said.

He walked to the impressive, room-size stone building and peered in through the iron-grated windows. The names of the occupants were etched in the marble slabs on the sides of the mausoleum.

"The Terrible Gennas," he said to himself, remembering the nickname for the Maxwell Street family that had provided Capone with horrible moonshine whiskey flavored with "fuel oil" and colored with coal tars.

Jim translated the names on the slabs into the men's nicknames:

Angelo Genna - "Bloody Angelo"
Anthony Genna - "Tony the Aristocrat"
Michael Genna - "Mike the Devil"

The other three Gennas, he could tell by the dates, had survived the bloody gang wars of the 1920s. They had done so by getting out of the city, and returning only years later.

Somewhere nearby, he knew, their bitter enemy, Dion

O'Bannion, was buried. Al Capone's gunmen murdered him in his flowershop across from Holy Name Cathedral.

Jim walked back to the car.

"That's the Genna brothers' mausoleum back, there," he told Janice. "They were gangsters who supplied Johnny Torrio and Al Capone with cheap whiskey." He felt a wince of death far away as he showed off his knowledge.

"Have you ever seen Mr. Capone's grave?" Janice asked.

Jim was surprised by her wording even more than the question. He was certain he had never ever heard Chicago's most infamous gangster referred to as "Mister" before.

"No," he answered.

"I'll show you."

Her directions took them in a circle around a hill in the very center of the winding drives. On top of it sat the largest mausoleum in the cemetery. This was reserved for the bodies of the Roman Catholic bishops and archbishops of Chicago. The structure itself, Jim thought, was more awful than awe-inspiring. The clumsy and bombastic style of architecture was a mixture of Greek and Bzyantine design.

"God," he said to himself.

Only then did he notice an angel with a trumpet on top of the mausoleum. From the ample breasts on the figure, he saw it was a female angel. If he remembered his religion lessons right, "her" name was Gabriel.

Following Janice's directions, Jim drove the car back almost to the gate of the cemetery and than veered left. A hundred yards down the roadway, she told him to stop. A few yards off the road, in a clump of attractively trimmed bushes, was a large, marble monument with the name "Capone" on it. It might be, he thought, the most attractive and understated monument in the cemetery.

Janice pointed to the ground in front of the monument. There, simple flat gravestones bore the names of the Capone family, starting with the father, Gabriel 1865 - 1920. Next was Al Capone's mother, Theresa 1865 - 1952. Then there was the gangster himself. His gravestone read:

Alphonse Capone
1899 - 1947
My Jesus Mercy

Next followed the markers for other Capone children such as Ralph, Vinzeno and Umberto. The words of a poem he had learned in grade school went through Jim's head:

Life is real. Life is earnest.
The grave is not its goal.
To dust thou shall returneth,
Was not spoken of the soul.

"Is there an afterlife," Jim wondered. "Did the nefarious and vicious deeds of a man like Capone catch up with him, not only when he was in the penitentiary and during the syphilitic state of his final days, but also after death?"

"After death, Janice, after death," he said. "That's what this place is all about. That's why the angel is on top the archbishops' mausoleum. She's up there waiting for Judgment Day. What a collection that angel is going to gather from this cemetery!"

"It will be interesting," Janice said simply.

"Janice, it doesn't work. This cemetery shows that any religious notion of the resurrection of the dead is as preposterous as the marble and cement tombstones in this place."

"It works if you believe, Mr. Rooney."

"Believe in what?"

"I guess in the Apostle's Creed." Jim was surprised at how pinpointed her answer was. It was straight out of the second grade catechism. The Apostle's Creed mentions the Trinity, the Church and even the resurrection of the dead.

"Janice," he challenged, "somehow nuns have got to fare a little better in a Catholic cemetery than mobsters like Al Capone. This monument to him and his family is beautiful and his own marker says, 'My Jesus Mercy'."

"Eddie says Mr. Capone was really O.K. He just wanted some things very badly and he took them. People resented that."

"Your Eddie scares me. Capone was a murderer. He personally decided when at least fifty other people would enter this cemetery. I don't understand you sometimes, Janice. You are a kind person, and yet you can accept your Eddie's sick morality."

"You're right Mr. Rooney. I get confused sometimes."

What Janice did not add was how frightened his comments made her. Eddie was beyond her understanding, especially when it came to his anger and his need to take revenge. And it was Janice whom Eddie was angry at now.

The ghost whose picture she had to show Jim Rooney was next.

૪

CHAPTER NINE

ςο

Sunset

Jim drove the car into the small Mount Carmel Cemetery office parking lot near the north entrance. Just south of the lot, a willow tree tickled the top of a large marble monument.

Getting out of his car and staring at the tree, Jim saw that the tombstone beneath bore the name, "Buccola." He walked toward it, shaking his head. Was he actually seeing something pertaining to one of Janice's ghosts?

As they neared it he could see that the white monument, about 12 feet in circumference, had both Italian and English words on it.

"This is it," Janice said, reconfirming what was obvious.

"Why am I here?" Jim asked himself. "This is all crazy."

It was all so different from covering a murder or a fire or a press conference, all specific events with reportable facts behind them.

"What has this girl got me doing?"

He had lent this young girl more faith than he had anyone in a long while. Why? He tried to recall the sequence of events. Then he remembered Paul Kowalski, Paul who was buried across Roosevelt Road in Queen of Heaven Cemetery.

"Cemeteries are for real," he said distractedly to Janice.

"You are thinking of someone buried near here," she said almost clairvoyantly.

"Yes, a very good friend."

There was silence. Jim thought of Paul. He remembered a surprise birthday party Paul had thrown for him. Jim loved cake and had jokingly complained to Paul that he never had gotten a big enough cake for his birthday. Paul, good old Paul, had bought an enormous wedding cake for Jim.

"I'm sorry, Janice," Jim said. "I was off somewhere. You have a ghost to show me."

She pointed to a photograph of a young woman in a wedding dress held in a glass frame permanently fastened to the upper half of the monument. Below it were inscribed the Italian words, *Offro questo dono a'mia cara figlia Giulia di anni 29.*

Janice had learned the translation and offered it, "I offer this gift to my dear 29-year-old daughter Julia."

Farther down on the monument was the photograph Janice had spoken of, the picture of Julia Buccola. It showed the young woman in the same wedding dress, lying in her coffin. There was dirt on the sides of the casket.

Next to the photo was an inscription, a strange mixture of Italian and English words: *Filumena Buccola Julia aged 29 Questa fotograha presa dopo 6 anni morti.*

Jim grasped that it stated that this photograph had been taken six years after Julia's death.

A feeling of goose-pimpled surprise went through Jim's body. Julia Buccola's body, according to the picture and inscription, had been preserved. Furthermore, the face of dead Julia was pale and puffy like that of the girl in Jim's dream.

He stared at her features, hoping to tell whether or not he had seen them in his dream. He simply could not decide.

"The story," Janice explained, "is that Julia's mother dreamed her daughter was a saint and that her body was preserved like some saints' bodies are. Her mother kept having this dream, so finally she had Julia's body dug up. The picture shows you what they found."

"Six years later?"

"Yes."

"How did she die? Why the wedding dress?"

"She died having the baby. The wedding dress, I was told, was just the way they dressed young mothers who died in childbirth back then."

"Is that all, Janice?"

"No. The baby was buried with Julia."

"Yes?"

"Yeah, but its body was not preserved." Jim walked around the monument and found the infant's name on the reverse side.

"Janice, interesting. But this really doesn't make Julia Buccola a ghost. I can't explain why her body didn't decompose, but she's no spirit walking about, and that's what ghosts supposedly are."

"Maybe you're wrong, Mr. Rooney. Maybe she does walk around."

"What do you mean?"

"A lot of people say they've seen her. People who don't know anything about the grave have seen her walking around the cemetery in her wedding dress."

"Like who?"

"One time, a five-year-old boy. He got left behind accidentally at the cemetery. He described her just perfect after the family came back to pick him up. Apparently, Julia was about ready to take his hand when his mother reached him."

"Those are stories, Janice."

"I know that. There's a high school over there—I can't remember its name—but when they have a dance, somebody claims to see Julia, and the whole dance will empty out as the kids flock to the fence to try to see her."

"That's because people want to believe."

"I know that because I do. I mean I just can't imagine not believing," she said.

Jim stood looking at the monument. The Italian inscriptions, the photographs, the cemetery, Janice herself—they were a different world. There was no sense to it all, even to the fact that he was here. But something told him to hold back judgment, at least for the moment. Perhaps it had been Julia's photo. Her face was very much like that of the girl in his dream—too much like it.

"Let's go, Janice," he mumbled. The two got in the car and headed south at Janice's request toward Archer Avenue. Jim wondered if he would be able to find the turn-around she had described. Once the car turned onto Archer Avenue, it became a moot question, as his attention was diverted to the wildness of the stretch. He had driven here many times in his life, but now he paid more attention to it. It was a strange street that belonged in another time, he thought, certainly in another location. Janice was a good navigator and warned him ahead of time where to stop the car. After she had him pull off the road, he stopped the vehicle and they got out.

Many of the leaves had fallen but the more stubborn ones still clung to the trees. It almost dark, but still light enough to show scraps of paper and pieces of litter mixed with leaves at their feet. This was wilderness, far more than he had expected.

"Is this where you heard music?" Jim asked.

"We were parked over there, but the music was all around us."

"Did you all hear it?"

"That's the funny thing," Janice said. "We all heard it. But now Eddie says he didn't. It's like something in his head or in his memory changed."

"What about the others?"

"Right now they ain't saying nothing. They get this dumb, 'Gee, I don't know' look. I get the feeling pretty soon they're going to start saying they didn't hear it."

"Do they lie?"

"We all do if Eddie wants us to or even if we think he does."

"I don't like your Eddie."

"You don't understand. He really has something special. Everybody sees that."

"Yeah, sure, Janice. About the music..."

"It was here."

"Janice, I have to ask you this. Was it really here? Did you honestly and truly hear it?"

"Yes, sir, it was. I get real chilled deep inside me every time I think about it. I mean it happened and it still scares me."

"Look Janice—I don't disbelieve you. I just suspend judgment when I hear about this kind of thing. I say, 'Well, maybe there's something we don't know.'"

"Maybe there is. It was so different, though. The music kinda hung up in the trees and like it came off the branches. If it could have broken glass, I guess it would've. It spooked me like nothing I ever heard or saw in my life."

"Right here?"

"You know right now I can't hear it, but I think maybe I feel it. Do you think that's possible?"

"Certainly not surprising, Janice. If you had a strong experience here, you could expect to recall it in some form when you come back the first time."

"Do you feel it, Mr. Rooney?"

"No. I do not. I feel something, just a little, but I don't think I can begin to say it is music."

"What do you feel?"

"I feel a little apprehensive, and I don't know why."

"I don't feel frightened. That music like opened a door for me. I didn't realize it till I came back here just now."

"What do you mean?"

"You know, I was caught or something and I didn't know it."

"You mean you aren't anymore?" he asked.

"Yes. But I know it now. It's like the door's there, but I can't walk through it yet. Do you think that was how it was for her?"

"Who?"

"For Mary."

"If you believe in Resurrection Mary, I guess you'd say it's still the way it is for her, a door that she can't walk through."

"Mr. Rooney, do you believe there is a Resurrection Mary?"

"Hardly," he said looking straight into her eyes. "I'm sorry. I wish you had not asked."

"I do," she said. "I believe. I think there is a reason for everything that is happening. I think we are going to meet her."

The wind rustled through the branches and the remaining leaves, creating a light orchestra of sounds. It wasn't music, much less Gregorian chant. They both knew that, but looking at each other, they began to smile

"Do you want to see where that boy was killed?" she asked.

"Maybe another time," he said.

"It's right down there."

"Are those the skid-marks?" he asked.

"Yes."

"Let's see them another time," Jim said. "We've had enough to do with dead people this evening."

&

CHAPTER TEN

ᔓ

Peoria State Hospital

Thursday afternoon, October 24

If Sarah could have magically changed one thing about herself, she would have developed an ease in knowing how to get started, it wouldn't have mattered on what. Just getting started on anything was difficult for her. Once she finally did, her confidence rose and she could take action. This she believed.

Buddy Wojcik—"Uncle Bud," actually her great uncle—was no help whatsoever to her in starting a conversation. His eyes stared blankly at the ground and his shoulders bent in agreement. Buddy, somewhere in his 90s, looked even older. Short and frail, he weighed not more than 100 pounds, even with his overcoat on.

"He's a dear, little old man," she thought. "So this is what you look like when you're almost 100." She tried to picture Ed at this age. She could picture his face wrinkled and his body bent over, but no matter how hard she tried to see him shriveled up, his chest and torso still appeared enormous.

Sarah could not resist the temptation of speculating, "Maybe someone this old has just lived too long. It certainly would be true if it happened to Ed."

Peoria State Hospital looked much like Uncle Bud, or was it the other way around? It dated, as he did, from before the turn of the century. The institution was made up of large old brick buildings on an extensive acreage, surrounded by a large stone and steel fence. Its curving walkways were broken occasionally by park benches. The clothes of the inhabitants showed their poverty, but even more clearly the insensitivity of the Illinois governors and legislators. This place, Sarah immediately knew, could use a good beauty shop, a boutique, or a bowling alley more than any additional psychologists or social workers.

Ed had not accompanied her onto the grounds of the hospital.

"At least there should be good whiskey in Peoria," he said. "They make the stuff here." With that, he left to find a bar. That sentence was all Ed had said in their last two hours of driving.

"But," she told herself, "that's probably more than I'll get out of Uncle Bud.

"Well," she said to Uncle Bud, "if you don't want to talk, that's all right. I'll do the talking." Sarah was tempted to swear like a riveter, to curse the Pope or talk about sex, just to see if she'd get her uncle to raise his eyes from the ground.

"Oh, hell," is what she settled for. It brought no reaction.

"This guy I'm with," she started jabbering to her strange companion, "you wouldn't believe him. He's a cop. Got a nice body. I'm interested in him. He's making like to leave me. Ah, Uncle Bud, what the hell do you understand about such things? Ma says you been in here almost forever.

"I'm sorry," she said, changing the tone of her voice. "I don't want to offend you. I mean I got a problem. I don't know how I get myself into these things. I ought to leave the ape. I mean if I was smart, that's what I'd do. I'd leave him. But then—the ache and the pain! You know what I mean, Uncle Bud?"

It was a rhetorical question, but surprisingly it brought from Uncle Bud a mumbled, "Yes. Understand."

A few minutes earlier the response would have startled Sarah. Now she was so into her own troubles that she chose not to hear his words. Her frustration spilled out.

"This guy is no good for me," she continued. "But what am I going to do? I like having a guy. I'm 38, and he's all I've got." She felt her throat tighten.

"What is it that binds the wrong people together so strong?" she asked. "I see this kind of thing all the time. If I had a nickel for every customer with this problem, I'd be one rich bitch. They want that bond, and then they find out they don't. That's what real pain is all about, if you ask me."

She looked at Uncle Bud. She wondered if his bent-over stance meant he was ducking some kind of pain, too. They continued moving step by slow step in silence along the state hospital paths that circle around the grounds. As they walked he used a cane and balanced his weight on his right arm. There was a firmness to his movement, a determination in his step that gave Sarah a sense of how he had survived. She had read a Sunday magazine article about Charles Darwin and his ideas about survival of the fittest.

"With human beings it has to be different," she thought, wondering how this frail old man could survive longer than physically developed men like Ed Wolinski.

Sarah tried to think of a way to describe her uncle. He was very different, very. He sent out odd vibrations. She recalled a phrase she had heard somewhere. She tried it out in her mind and it seemed to fit him. It was the term "wrapped in silence." Moments passed. She shared the silence. But she was not used to quiet.

"Why'd I tell you all those things about Ed?" Sarah asked Uncle Bud. "It was crazy to come here. I don't know why I did it in the first place. I wish I hadn't," she said, trying to cover her embarrassment at having revealed herself. Sarah looked at her watch. Even if he kept his promise, which, at this point, she had little reason to believe he would do, Ed would not be back for another half an hour.

"Can I get a cab around here?" she asked her uncle.

The old man did not answer. In frustration she ran her hand through her curly red hair.

"Uncle Bud, I'm sorry I'm treating you this way, I mean, like you don't even exist. Jeez, I have a very fond memory of you, you know that? I remember coming here as a little girl, and you held me on your lap. My folks were going through their divorce at the time. I remember telling my Ma that I always could run off and live with Uncle Bud. 'They have lots of bed there,' I said."

There was no response from her uncle.

"You know what, Uncle Bud," she continued, "I'll bet you're an expert on psychology. I mean, them psychologists and psychiatrists been working on you ever since you came here. I'll bet you know more about it than they do."

The old man did not acknowledge her comments.

"Hey, you know what? I'm a pretty good psychologist myself. You know what I did? Let me tell you. Ed wanted his son, Eddie, to get married. Only the kid hates the old man, and there ain't no way he is going to do what his father wants him to. So I tell him, 'Ed, offer the kid a car if he doesn't marry the girl.' Guess what? The kid does just what I tell Ed he'll do. Only this Eddie doesn't ask—he tells the girl to marry him. So everybody's happy. So I made everybody happy. Well, that's not exactly right. I'm kind of worried about what I got the girl into."

"Uncle Bud, what do you care about the story I'm telling you?" she said, sighing.

"So guess what happens then?" she tried again. "The girl goes off with some newspaper guy searching for a young girl who's some kind of ghost in a cemetery."

At that moment, the electricity in the air changed, or at least Sarah's sense of it did. Her uncle's body suddenly shivered and creaked to life.

Uncle Bud spoke. His voice, hollow and deep, was distinct and surprisingly loud.

"What was name." It was not a question. It was a demand. Still, he did not look up.

"The girl?" she responded. "Her name I think is Janice."

"No," her uncle asked impatiently. "The ghost?"

"The ghost?" The question didn't make sense to Sarah.

"Name!" It was, even more clearly than before, a demand.

"Oh, the ghost's name," she said, finally grasping his question, but stunned at this dialogue with her uncle.

"Yes—ghost's name," he said again.

"Resurrection Mary," she answered.

There were several moments of silence.

"Tell them come here," he finally said.

"Who?"

"Girl and reporter."

"Why?"

"They find her here."

"Who?"

"Resurrection Mary."

"What are you talking about, Uncle Bud?"

"Sarah," he said, stunning her by using of her name. "Knew the girl you call Resurrection Mary. She ... reason here."

Sarah was embarrassed without knowing why. She was also sad for her uncle.

So this was the family secret! She remembered hearing some mention about Uncle Bud and ghosts. She recalled her mother's not letting her repeat the story of Resurrection Mary when she was a teenager, but none of the pieces had come together. She was not certain they had now. Uncle Bud, no matter what his problem was, was certainly something different. She was even less comfortable now with him. They talked no more.

"Well, you knew he was crazy," she said to herself.

That evening

"Rooney, write a Halloween story for Sunday. Make it about 15 inches. Write about Chicago ghosts. I understand you are from the Southwest Side, and they have ghosts out there."

He stared at Busby, who just had given him the assignment. Jim's memo on the Southwest Side had come to this. His column, he thought, was not to be, and this was the way he was being told.

Sometimes, Jim believed, reporters can be as big and as

important as stories they cover. Then there are moments such as this. He was compromised. He had wanted the story of Resurrection Mary to be special, to be given his best as a researcher and a writer. It had possibilities, and he felt good about them. Now, however, he would have to crank out a story covering the same territory and do it in two hours. One of the versions would have to be shortchanged, possibly both of them.

His column was not to be. Ah, he could find a new angle to use on that. He was disappointed, but it was the problem of having to do the story of Resurrection Mary before it was ready that bothered him.

A single word came into his head. It entered from he knew not where. It rattled around and, not associated with anything else.

The word was "Punt." Paul used to say it all the time. "Paul...the letter!"

He would get the editor to reprint Paul's article and, along with it, the reader's letter.

"Thanks," he said, not quite knowing whom he was thanking.

3 P.M., Friday, October 25

Ed Wolinski did not like downstate Illinois. Chicago born and bred, he was accustomed to buildings, expressways, and congestion. His peripheral vision wanted to watch for a car accident, a crime, or a confrontation, not a stand of oak trees trying to create a silhouette or 40 acres of tanned cornstalks that still pointed bleakly to the sky although they had cumulatively given up trying to reach it. The highways of Illinois took him through farmland and more farmland. They crossed rivers and undeveloped lands that were a mixture of marshes and woods. For several hundred miles south of Peoria, the landscape continued to be flat, and made little impression on Ed. His responses were those of an animal, a nervous one, far away from his usual hunting grounds.

Even though Sarah had yet to reach her goal, she knew now the trip was a mistake. She had stopped telling herself that things would get better on the trip. With a compulsiveness she had not witnessed before, Ed was raising his brown paper bag to his mouth and gulping down whiskey. His grumbling was slurred and his comments toward her, short and mean. She could not go for a walk or to a movie to avoid his barbs as she usually did at home.

Uncle Clete lived outside the town of Okawville, in a dreary area where the backwaters of the Kaskaskia River lay stagnant in the ditches. There was nothing for miles in any direction and for very good reason. His place was several miles up a back-road. A cousin, a teacher in Herrin, had told her how to get out there, saying, "It's quite a'ways northwest of here. If nowhere has a focal point, Old Clete lives there—if you can call it living."

Her uncle Clete, far more paranoid than Uncle Bud in the state mental hospital, had chosen this secluded site "so the Sheltons won't find me," long after the last of the Shelton gang had disappeared from Williamson County, which was miles away.

"Nobody would want to find anybody here," Sarah had said impatiently, driving up the back-road. At times, she was not certain there was a road anywhere in front of her. Ed was snoring.

The shack in which her Uncle Clete lived came up suddenly.

"My god!" she gasped.

The house, more a shanty, was worse than what she had seen on the ridges in the back-hills of Kentucky. It was ready to fall down. The boards were weather-beaten and warped. The one-room cabin once had been wrapped in tarpaper, but the warp of the boards had broken through it. The yard smelled of stale water. Grasses and weeds grew wild where there were no tire rims or abandoned cars to crowd them aside. The cars, cans, pieces of sheet metal and even old magazines scattered about the premises had all been used for target practice.

Uncle Clete stood in the center of it with a rifle aimed at the car. His stubby whiskers were tobacco-stained. His eyes and mouth scrunched together in angry defiance. His longjohns—he wore no shirt—were filthy. He was, it seemed to Sarah, more a caricature than a person.

He growled what she understood to be a mumbled curse.

"Uncle Clete," she said with an attempted dignity. "It's little Sarah—used to live with my Grandma Sepe.

"Becky's dead," he snarled.

"Well, I ain't," she answered.

"Whadyawant?" he snapped.

"Just to talk," she said, "talk about the hanging and the old days."

"You a Sepe, then y'er kin," he answered gruffly. "Got to watch out for the Sheltons."

A woman in her late 50s came out of the cabin. Sarah was startled by her physical similarity to the haggard-faced woman who had posed for the American Cancer Society poster to discourage people from smoking. She chewed on a pipe instead of a cigarette.

"That's my woman, Nora," he said to Ed.

Sarah could not keep from contrasting in her mind the two uncles she had encountered on this trip. Uncle Bud had a bad case of institutional poverty. His coat was the wrong size and style and it was threadbare. But both he and the coat were clean. Uncle Clete was not.

She did not want to go inside the shack. She did not even want to see what was there. Sarah, painfully repulsed, planned to leave. She did not feel even a need, much less a desire, to be polite.

"We have to go," she announced.

"No, we don't," Ed countered. Sarah was stunned. Ed was fascinated with her Uncle Clete. Her companion stared at her uncle with a smile, almost a silly grin on his face. His eyes were eager, like those of a 12-year-old listening to a dirty story. The old man was mean, petty, foul-mouthed and long-winded, and Ed wanted to hear every detail that he had to give.

They leaned against an early 1930s automobile, garbage-strewn and tireless in the front yard. The subject quickly got to the 1920s. Ed pumped her uncle for the gory details of everything he might have seen or done in which violence was connected. Clete had been 16 years old when he witnessed the 1920s massacre by a brutal mob against the men working in the mines as scabs in Herrin. He had also knew about the shooting of vigilante law enforcer Clyde Young. He spoke of bullet holes oozing blood and of flies around dead bodies kicked by the women and children, including himself

"They did, eh?" Ed asked. The eagerness and attentiveness of his listener brought a light to Clete's eyes and a curl to his upper lip that made him look even more gross. He spoke with macabre zest of the hanging of his pal, Charlie Birger, which he had witnessed. Ed started to counter with brutal things he had seen and some he had done as a cop.

"It used to be when we got a guy in the station," he said, "we could get anything out of him. God, you don't how good a rubber hose can feel in your hand. I mean it doesn't leave marks, especially on niggers."

"Yeah, it were a lot of fun to beat up one of them. God, they got uppity with the war." Uncle Clete elaborated with a brutal story of a lynching in which a white mob was "only defending the honor of our wimmen".

"Wimmen get uppity, too," Nora said in a gravel voice. That sentence, Sarah later recalled, were the only words Nora uttered during the whole visit.

"We got ways for them, too," Ed said. "Some of them aggressive ones, they like to be frisked, you know that? In Chicago, we get 'em in the station, and we make 'em strip." Sarah stopped listening and let her mind wander back to Uncle Bud. Ed had told her such things before and she had refused to let them bother her. Now, however, they were spewing out in the context of the life of her repulsive uncle. While Ed regaled her uncle, Sarah looked again at Nora.

"I'm going for a walk, a long one," she said, taking a deep breath.

"Stay here," Ed ordered.

Sarah ignored the command. She walked into the woods, pushing aside the scrubby bushes as she went, her head arched high.

In her muscles, heart, and mind, she felt disconnected from the three people she had just left, rid of them, free, above all, from the bonds to the man she had brought to Southern Illinois.

The relationship was over. She knew she did not want or need a man who would wind up like Uncle Clete and turn her into his "woman."

In the relationship, Sarah had dammed up a river of things she now, suddenly, regretted. She felt the torrent of them gushing to the surface.

"I'm no better than they are," she said, and then stopped herself.

Floating in the middle of her memory was the thought that she had suggested that Ed use reverse psychology on his son to get him married. It all looked different now. It was the girl whom she saw so clearly now. That helpless young thing would be getting another Ed in the deal, and it would be her fault.

"You only got one more thing to do with that man," she resolved. "You got to level with that girl about what you did to her, and maybe, just maybe, tell her the stuff that Uncle Bud had said."

Sarah started running through the scrubby woods. With her arms spread and the exhilaration of a child released for recess, she began yelling, "Red Rover, Red Rover, let Sarah come over!"

☙

CHAPTER ELEVEN

༄

Sunday evening, October 27

"Hello, is this Janice O'Leary?"

"Yes."

"I not sure how to start this conversation. But, my name is Sarah Winecki. I'd like to meet you and talk."

"Do I know you?" Janice asked. "Are you the one who gave that plastic dishes demonstration I went to once? I don't think I want any."

"No, Janice," the woman on the phone said, laughing. "I'm not selling anything."

"I'm sorry, ma'am. You don't know how people who sell stuff like that can be. I thought like you were one of them. They can really keep after you."

"I know, I can't like them either. What I want to talk to you about is Eddie and somebody you're looking for."

"I ain't looking for anybody."

"I was told you were."

"Who?"

"Resurrection Mary."

"How do you know that I—I mean that like we were looking for her? And about Eddie, how do you know that?"

"Janice, I know a lot of things. Could you meet me after school tomorrow at Gertie's, say about 3:30? Or, if not, some other time?"

"No—that's fine..."

"Good, Janice. It's important. It really is."

Gertie's was a turn of the century ice cream parlor at Kedzie Avenue and 59th Street, a hang-your-cap place. It had originally been surrounded by farm houses and little else. Gertie's reputation was based on the fact that it made fresh ice cream early every morning. Southwest Siders used it for dates, after-movie snacks, and family treats. What Sarah wanted to say was necessary, but would be upsetting to Janice. Gertie's, she felt, would be a reassuring atmosphere.

Sarah pegged Janice instantly. Among the after-school crowd in the wooden-boothed store, only one girl sat by herself.

"I'll say one thing," Sarah began. "This place brings back memories. I take it you've been here before, too?"

"Yes, I have. I don't think I know you. You don't look like the saleslady at all. You're pretty."

"I have a little trouble believing that."

"No, you really are. Your name is Sarah, did you say?"

"Right. Can I ask you something about Eddie first. Are you two getting along real good?"

"Well, he is very angry with me, but we are engaged."

"Do you want to marry him?"

"It ain't that simple."

"Are you afraid of him?"

"I never told anybody this before, but, yeah, I am."

"I don't know if what I'm going to tell you is gonna hurt you or not. I think it's gonna help, or I wouldn't do it."

"Why are you saying all this, ma'am?"

"You got a right to ask that. I am, or rather I was, Eddie's father's girlfriend."

"I always thought he had one. Eddie won't talk about it. He just doesn't talk about his family. I've met his mother a lot of times. She's nice. I think Junior once told me Eddie's father had a girlfriend."

"That 'had' is the right word. It's over, I'm happy to say."

"What do you want from me?" Janice squirmed, unsure of Sarah's motives.

"I want to tell you a couple of things, Janice. I don't know how... I guess if you really want to marry him, I shouldn't be telling you."

"I'm engaged to Eddie, but I really don't know if I want to marry him. Maybe I shouldn't talk about it?"

"Maybe you should."

"Eddie, well, sometimes he hits me. Maybe if we were married he wouldn't."

"Sounds like what we women always tell ourselves."

"I get awfully bored. Eddie ain't boring."

"Then I am going to tell you, Janice, why Eddie wants to marry you. It's because he thinks his father wants him not to do it."

"What?"

"It gets worse. Eddie's mother talked to a priest. He told her Eddie would mellow out if he got married."

"I dunno. Maybe he would."

"Let me tell you. I thought I was going to reform my Jules. All I ever did was give him a target for his fists. So now I'm gonna tell you what I have to."

"Please..."

"Ed wanted his son to get married. It was because his wife wanted it. I said to Ed he ought to tell Eddie not to marry you. And that, if Eddie didn't marry you, he would buy him a car. I knew it'd make Eddie mad and make him want to marry you out of spite for his old man."

"What?"

"Eddie hates his old man—really hates him. That's what's wrong with him. I knew Eddie'd do the exact opposite of what his father told him to do. It's just that it was my idea, and now I feel bad about it."

"Eddie can be very bull-headed. Isn't that reverse psychology or something?"

"Yeah, it is. You know, you sound like you don't care."

"Well, you're right. I feel like my life's been, like plotted. I'm kinda glad to know it's been true rather than just something in my head. I don't have to do something that I was supposed to. Your telling me sort of helped. Thanks."

"I didn't do you any favor, Janice."

"I'm sorry. I have to think about this."

Sarah murmured a reassuring agreement.

"You said something else on the phone, something about Resurrection Mary." Janice looked up at Sarah and grinned. "I can't believe how much better I feel about the thing with Eddie."

"Ed told me you and some reporter guy were going in search of her," Sarah smiled and said.

"That's true."

"Well, this is crazy, but my Uncle Bud told me he danced with her."

"You're kidding! That's what we're been looking for."

"Wait, Janice, there's a problem."

"Don't worry about it. Mr. Rooney said that all we needed was somebody who'd met her."

"Janice, I said that there's a problem."

"What is it?"

"My uncle, he's in this place. It's a mental institution."

"Oh boy! What's wrong with him?"

"He's an old man in his 90s and he's kind of senile."

"Is he looney?"

"Janice, he knows something. I wouldn't pass this on to you if he was simply looney. I mentioned you and your reporter to him. He asked to see you. He's at Peoria State Hospital. I'd like to see you go."

"That's up to Mr. Rooney. You know what?"

"What?"

"I like you."

"Oh, honey, you don't know how good that makes me feel. I just lost a man I thought could be my friend."

"Eddie's dad?"

"Yeah. You know he hit me sometimes, too. And I still wanted him awful bad. I don't anymore. I guess that's how I got the courage up to talk to you. What are you going do about Eddie?"

"I dunno. What should I do?"

"Right now, I don't know. But if you ever need to talk,

give me a call." Sarah scribbled down her phone number on the napkin in front of her and pushed it over to Janice.

"Thanks."

"And, let me know how it works out with my uncle."

"I promise."

"Have that reporter call me and I'll give him the details. Try to convince him to go."

"OK, I'll try."

Theodore's bookstore

Late Wednesday afternoon, October 30

"Young man," Theodore said, "You have been loitering here for half an hour. I seriously doubt you have come here to buy a book. What is it that you want?"

"Nothing," Eddie Wolinski answered.

"Unless you have something better than nothing to look for, please don't stay around here."

"Naw don't worry about me, old man. I'm looking for a guy. I hear this guy's a friend of yours, and he hangs out here."

"No one, as you put it, 'hangs out' here. This is not a drive-in. For whom are you looking?"

"Guy by the name of Jim Rooney. A reporter."

"You have come to the right place, albeit with the wrong attitude."

"'Albeit, with the wrong attitude.' You talk awful big. I ain't impressed."

"I'm from the Back of Yards. If I were younger, I'd wipe you up with more than language."

"Well, you ain't younger. Where's this big deal reporter at? I hear he's tall and skinny and wears glasses."

"Young man, I would tell you he also looks like Joyce, but that would be way above you."

"That's where you're wrong, old man. I've read some James Joyce stuff. I know what he looked like."

"Why didn't Joyce have a civilizing influence on you?"

"You figure it out, 'cause I already have. Ya gotta want to be what you call 'civilized.' And I don't want to be. Put that in your pipe and smoke it."

"I think I shall. Thank you."

"Whadya thankin' me for?"

"Because I am going to do just what you told me to do. Put it my pipe and smoke it. I don't think I've ever met anyone quite like you. I tend to think some people are not more civilized human beings because they have not had contact with the noble thinking in good books. I need to be reminded sometimes that there are also people like you."

"Confuse you, don't I?"

"Not entirely. You just remind me there aren't any formulas. I need that reminder. Why are you looking for Jim Rooney?"

"That's my business."

"Well, my business is books, and perhaps I should just not indulge you in yours."

"I don't care."

"Still, I will tell you. He comes here before work. He should be here at 4:30. About another half hour."

"Hey, old man, I don' think you or I dig each other. So what say I wait outside?"

"A most agreeable suggestion for my part. I find your 'old man' bit rather abrasive, which is probably why you bother to do it."

"You haven't got me all figured out, old man, so don't try."

"I shall do as I want, as I'm sure we both shall. May I have your name?"

"No. What kind of car does this Rooney drive anyway?"

"A 1964 light blue Chevy, I believe."

"If you think I'm going to thank you for your help, don't."

"I am willing to suggest something to help you. I will sell you a book on Nietzsche so you can see you are not the first one to espouse your negative philosophy."

"No thanks. If I wanted one of your books, I'd steal it. And I'll tell you my name because you stopped asking. It's Eddie."

"You steal from me and I'll have you in jail with a bunch

of other fellows who have similar attitudes toward society."

"They do except they're dumb—they got caught. If I wanted that book, I'd have someone else take it for me."

"I feel sorry for you. And I'm beginning to worry about my friend, James, if he is going to have any dealings with you."

"Then I got you where I want you."

"Leave the store. I don't like someone who wallows his way through life to do so in the presence of my books."

"To someone so high and mighty, everyone must look like they're wallowing."

Theodore expected his guard to go down and his body to relax when Eddie left. It didn't, and his face was troubled a half hour later when Jim Rooney walked in.

"Did you meet him?" Theodore asked.

"Meet whom?"

"That obnoxious boy."

"What was his name?"

"Eddie. He was here looking for you."

"That must be Janice's boyfriend. No, I didn't run into him. From what Janice has told me about him, he certainly seems to be rather brutal."

"I had a most unpleasant encounter with this Eddie. He said he was going to wait to see you. He didn't seem to be the kind who gives up easily."

"Tell me about it."

"If he called me 'old man' one more time, I would have let him have it."

"My, my, Theodore, I hope you never get angry with me."

"He told me if he wanted one of my books, he'd have someone else steal it for him. He wouldn't even be man enough to do it himself."

"I know. One of the nice things about this quest for Resurrection Mary is that it is pulling Janice away from him."

"Do you think that's why he was waiting to see you? He probably wants to punch you out."

"I don't think so. From what I hear, he has other people do his dirty work."

"I think he is mad at you."

"Sure he is. He thinks Janice is his chattel and that I am freeing her."

"You got a mean punk on your hands."

"Don't worry about it. If I survived Chicago's finest during the convention, I can outlast Eddie. I wonder what he wanted and why."

"He was so deliberate."

"Forget him for a while. I have some interesting news. Janice called me and said a friend gave her the name of a man in Peoria State Hospital who claims to have danced with Resurrection Mary."

"In the mental hospital?"

"My first reaction, too. But at last we have a name. I called the woman. This lady, her name is Sarah, believes her uncle really does know something."

"Peoria State Hospital?"

"Please, Theodore. Tomorrow we're going to drive down there."

"Maybe you belong there, James."

"You told me you had a feeling about this quest."

"But Peoria State Hospital? What's the patient's name?"

"Buddy Wojcik."

"Bingo! James, bingo, bingo, bingo!" Theodore's voice sounded jubilant. "That's it! Remember, I told you there were two names I heard as a kid? One was Mary. The other was Bud!"

"Anything else? Do you remember anything else, Theodore?"

"No. Nothing."

Across the street and partially hidden from the bookstore, Eddie occasionally glanced at the two men, watching to make sure they did not see him or what he was doing. He finished his task in about five minutes. Then, he walked slowly and deliberately past the front window of the store.

"I wish the hot shot reporter would take that old man bookdealer for a ride in his car," Eddie thought.

10 P.M. Wednesday, October, 30

"You're a son of son a bitch, Eddie," Junior said. "Your father is a son of a bitch and you're his son."

Junior never would have made such a statement to Eddie if it were not meant to be flattering. His mind always carefully distilled each word into a complimentary form. Even when Junior tried to protect Eddie and himself from Eddie's fury, he expressed his comments as homage. He hoped Eddie would accept this exclamation as praise. Junior knew he was on thin ice bringing up Eddie's father. That usually caused his friend to erupt.

Eddie, without responding, stared at a distant spot on the horizon. What he had done had been satisfying.

Junior, as usual, sensed that Eddie had done something big, even gone too far, an act bordering on cataclysmic. Eddie's silence, his smirk, his distance all said it, but Junior did not know what it was. He knew Eddie was ruthless and that Janice, with whom Eddie had been deeply angry, was now in danger. Junior cared little about her. In any other situation, Janice's safety might have meant something to Junior. He, however, only wanted Eddie's approval. His responsibility was to protect Eddie from the consequences of his own actions far more than to help or save Janice or anyone else.

"Eddie, whadyado?" Junior asked as nonchalantly as he could. His companion smiled. Eddie now could relax and enjoy for the first time the ruthlessness of his plot and feel of power involved in dealing life and death.

"I didn't do nothing," Eddie answered. "Like you said, I'm the son of a son of a bitch. If something was done, my old man did it." His father had set in motion the chain of events by being who he was. Any ruthless or mean thing Eddie had done had a satisfying face, for somehow his father could be blamed for it.

"What? Whadyado? Or, like, what'd yer old man do?"

To Eddie, knowledge was power. He was not about to give

up either. Junior sensed that, but persevered.

"You did something that will punish Janice and get that reporter," Junior persisted. "You know how I know? You stopped bitching, and you stopped figuring in your head. So I know you did something."

Eddie shrugged.

"It's going to happen soon," Junior probed. "A time bomb. You set some kind of a time bomb. No. That's not it, but it was something like that."

"I'm going for some sliders," Eddie said.

He never suggested, "Let's go." or "Let's do it." Eddie never even used the words, "we" or "us".

Junior, behind the wheel, started the car.

"The ignition. You did something to that guy's ignition. No. Not the ignition, but you did something to the car. That's it, his car! Right, Eddie?"

Junior was amazed at his own intuition, and he knew he was on target.

"Shaddup, Junior!"

Eddie's reaction was immediate. He very rarely called a companion or anyone else by his or her first name. Calling Junior by name was Eddie's way of complimenting his friend for having figured out so much. It was also meant to end the discussion.

Junior was frightened. Eddie had taken him down this path before, but this time he had gone much farther. The terrain was familiar, yet it was not.

Eddie, Junior knew, believed in revenge. Retaliation was a tight cord with which Eddie demanded loyalty. Sometimes he only threatened retaliation, but the worst of all crimes, to Eddie, was disloyalty.

Usually, Eddie had another member of his group carry out the retaliation, especially if it would hurt someone close to that person. Once he made Nancy punish her little brother in a way that caused her brother to lose his girlfriend. Eddie ordered her to tell a secret her brother confided in her. She protested, but later apologized to Eddie for questioning his judgment.

Junior knew he had to do something, not to protect Janice but to save Eddie from the consequences of his plot. Junior determined to call Janice and to warn her. He did not know what he would say, but he had to alert her. If only he knew more about what Eddie had done to the reporter's car.

Eddie sensed that Junior's questions meant he might be tempted to interfere.

"I loosened the bolts on the rear wheel of the guy's car," Eddie said, knowing full well that the best way to control Junior was to bring his companion in on the conspiracy.

"Goddamn it, Eddie, that's the biggest thing you've ever done," Junior said, breaking into a nervous smile.

"This time I got to the babushka first," Eddie said in a mock German voice.

Junior knew now he would not and could not call Janice, not if he valued Eddie's relationship.

"The babushka?" he questioned. Junior himself did not know what his own question meant.

Eddie seemed to grasp it, however, and responded, "Never mind."

ↈ

CHAPTER TWELVE

ೲ

Thursday afternoon, October 31

Jim adjusted his spectacles, pushing them tighter on the bridge of his nose as he leaned forward to look at the deeply slouched man whom the Peoria State Hospital attendant was bringing into the visitors' room to meet with him and Janice.

Buddy Wojcik, as Sarah had said, appeared to be "somewhere around 100, at least." His hair, uncombed and thin, was very white. Bent low, he did not, and physically could not, meet his visitors' eyes with his own. His spotted and wrinkled skin looked like that of a new-born piglet with blotches. Draped over his frame was a plaid suit-coat that once had fit someone 30 pounds heavier and three inches taller. It initially had two more buttons in front.

Buddy Wojcik stared at a spot on the ground in front of him, his head following the tilt of his shoulders.

Seeing before him what seemed the most fragile of human shells, Jim leaned down even farther as the old man opened his mouth and started to speak. All of Uncle Bud's appearance alerted Jim to expect to hear the mumbled words of a weak old man. Instead, a voice surprisingly strong jolted the reporter back to an upright stance.

"You come to talk 'bout Mary Waskowski."

It was a statement, not a question.

"Waskowski! Mary Waskowski!" In all the versions of the Resurrection Mary story Jim had heard, he had never before heard a last name.

"Will tell you 'bout Mary," the Peoria State Hospital

inmate continued in a voice that suddenly broke off in confusion, "but there is something else to tell you. What is? Don't 'member what is. Must. Must 'member."

The ancient man constantly skipped words, especially the personal pronoun "I", but his strong voice and deliberate enunciation carried his message nonetheless. His agitation, however, had become so pronounced that Jim feared he might not continue.

"It's all right," Jim assured him. "It's all right."

"No. Not all right. Do not 'member, but must tell you."

"Please continue. Tell me about meeting Mary Waskowski."

The mention of her name brought more relaxed breathing from the stooped figure.

"Long time since tell anybody," he began. "It was in old neighborhood. People have outdoor toilet. That was long ago. You know where toilet was? Under sidewalk. Nobody believe 'bout them."

"I know about the sidewalks," Jim smiled. "Joe Pudzievalkiem. Right?"

"Hey, you know Joe Pudzievalkiem?"

"Yes."

"*Yac Samash?*"

"No. I don't speak Polish, but I had a Polish friend who told me about Joe. I know when they elevated the grade in the old neighborhoods of Chicago, they put in rooms under the sidewalk. In Polish, they were *pudzievalkiem,* which means under the sidewalk. The space is where the outhouses were.

"You not Polish, but all right," the stooped figure said without attempting to look up. "Got to 'member what was supposed to tell."

The repetition of that phrase made Jim anxious. He was abrupt in reminding the elderly man about his place in the tale of Resurrection Mary, "You were talking about the old neighborhood."

"Knew Mary. Was in same catechism class. Made First Communion together."

"You knew her?"

This was not the story he had come to hear. That someone had known her was not part of the legend.

"Yes. In school, make First Communion together. She was older. Mary's parents were old country, not let her make communion until she was older than rest."

"How long ago was that?"

"Not ask. Know when it was. Now, not know when it is. Not want to."

It was the clearest statement yet of the old man's confused mental state, Jim judged.

"You know 'bout hearse?" the ancient man queried.

"What about the hearse?"

"Family was old country. People, modern for funerals in Chicago. Rich use hearse, and poor ride special 'L' car. Coffin lifted up to 'L' tracks at stops, and whole funeral go by 'L' to cemetery."

"And Mary's family did not approve?"

"They got special black oak hearse with glass sides from out in country, from Shakers or Holy Rollers or somebody. They hitch up to four horses."

"Then the family was wealthy?"

Buddy Wojcik waited to answer.

"Family strange," he said.

He coughed, wheezed, then started coughing hard.

Finally he spoke. The words did not come easily: "They have money, own bunch of houses. Parents crazy tight with money."

"How did Mary die?"

The old man coughed again.

"You not know how she die?"

"No. I don't."

"Mary Waskoswki die of poison."

"How?"

"She eat cabbage rolls with rat poison on them."

"What?"

"Her parents beat her and she run away from home. She come back hungry and eat out of garbage. They put poison in garbage to kill rats but not tell her."

"That's awful, awful. What were they punishing her for?" Janice asked.

"For spending nickel to go to dance. 'I will teach you to waste money!' Those last words her mother say to her. They always punish her when she wanted to spend money."

"Well, they didn't mean to kill her," Jim said.

"No, they want to keep her prisoner. She want to be free," Buddy Wojcik said.

Janice suddenly sat down.

"Mary, smart girl. She understand their craziness and knew she was their prisoner, but not get free."

"She had never rebelled until then?"

"She, Chicago Polish girl. Other girls rebel. They wind up whores. Last minute, before she die, Mary protest with curse."

Janice gasped.

"Parents tell priest. You know what? He not give them forgiveness. They, very cruel. Try to fool people with big funeral and headstone."

"There is a headstone?"

"No. People take it away in night. They call it sacrilege."

"But what about the dance?"

"You ask about dance? Always, they ask about it."

"Mr. Wojcik, did you dance with Mary Waskowski? Do you maintain it was after she was dead and buried?" the reporter in Jim challenged.

"Yes. Did dance."

"How do you know it was she, Mary Waskowski?"

"Always knew it Mary."

"But in the legend the young man goes to see her mother afterwards, and then he learns who it was."

"That not how it happen, but yes, go see her mother, go next day."

"Tell me about the dance."

"Saturday night. It is just before Advent dance at church. Not good dancer. Very shy. Want to meet girl. But not want to try to dance. See her. Scared. But she sad, and she ask. Good Polish girl not ask boy."

"Did you know right away it was Mary Waskowski, who

was supposed to be dead?"

"Oh, yes, know."

"Did she know you?"

"She know. She use Polish nickname only called when little boy."

"Were you frightened?" Janice asked.

"Yes. Felt she going to take with her. Felt going to die."

The room for a moment seemed filled with a settling silence. No one moved. And then a patient in an adjoining room groaned.

Jim, who had been performing the roll of interviewer with quick confidence, sensed a temporary loss of his easy certainty as the silence continued.

"Supposed to tell you somethin'," the ancient little man said.

Jim raised his eyebrows but ignored the distracting comment. He had pulled out his notebook and had started to scratch down phrases.

"How did she dance?" he asked.

"Awkward. Mary Waskowski not know how to dance."

"And after the dance?"

"She take to streetcar. Transfer twice. Go to Resurrection Cemetery. Not think coming back."

"Did she just leave you there?"

"No. She give small black box with ribbon around it.
"'Take it to the woman,' she say."

"The woman?" Jim quizzed. "Who did she mean?"

"Knew. Mean her mother."

"And did you?"

"Took it to her."

"What did she do?"

"She scream. 'That ribbon ... from Mary's hair!'"

"Then what?"

"She open box. In it is yellow hair."

"Yes?

"Her mother throw things."

"You gave her the lock of hair?"

"No. She not take."

"What happened to it?"

Buddy Wojcik fumbled in his shirt pocket and pulled out a small black, wooden box. Affixed to it was a faded, dusty lilac ribbon, whose edges still showed traces of the bright purple color it once was. He offered it to Jim.

"Here. You take."

Jim recoiled from taking the strange item. Without a word, Janice reached and took it.

She opened it reverently. It was there, the lock of a ghost's hair, at least according to this ancient mental patient. It was there, a physical part of the girl who had died of poison at the age of 15 allegedly some 80 or 90 years before, the girl whom Chicago knew as Resurrection Mary.

The reporter looked at the old man, who had a tear sliding down his left cheek.

"And then you came here?" the reporter asked.

"People knew. They knew 'bout dance with her, 'bout dance with girl they call 'Resurrection Mary.' They make fun or they afraid."

Janice, without saying a word, took the locket of blonde hair and matched it against her own.

Jim Rooney smiled in the realization that he had what he had set out for, a story. That's what it was. Not facts, a story, one so delicate that another word from the old man might fracture it. The legend was over. He felt only a touch of the elderly man's tragedy and loneliness, but he could describe them. Maybe the telling of the story in the paper would help Buddy Wojcik bury Resurrection Mary once and for all.

"It's a good story," Jim mused. "It doesn't matter that it is not true." He nodded and signaled his young companion it was time to leave.

Janice hesitated a moment and then hugged the old man, but said nothing. The short, bent figure half-jumped backwards, startled by the hug. He stared and appeared confused at the touch of the girl.

As they were driving away, the bent, old figure scurried to the window and looked out. He tapped on it in frustration. Buddy Wojcik tried to call out to them. They could not hear.

"Member, now. Member what to say."

Buddy spoke toward the floor, "Archer Avenue."

Evening, October 31

"It all started here," Jim thought to himself, as he turned the car onto Archer off the expressway. There had been an accident, and he had been assigned by the newspaper to follow up on the story. And it was here on Archer Avenue that Janice had heard the requiem music.

Jim had his Resurrection Mary story. It would write itself. Perhaps he would just print the old man's narrative as an interview or dialogue. He felt a glow. With this story, things at the newspaper could start breaking right for him.

He brushed back his hair from his forehead as he thought about Buddy Wojcik and the young Polish girl he had described. If only his editors would not interfere with his presentation of it, the tale could be told as a simple one. He wanted readers to share Buddy Wojcik's feelings, or rather his experiences. Jim knew he would fight to keep it a straight story that unraveled itself. Reporters rarely get the opportunity to write such pieces.

"You all right?" he asked Janice.

"I would of escaped," she said.

"What?" he asked.

"I would of found a way to leave, to escape," Janice said.

Darkness lay heavy on Archer Avenue. Jim scarcely noted the entrance to ancient St. James Sag Church and Cemetery. They had not yet come to the place where Janice had heard the music and where she had asked him whether or not he believed in Resurrection Mary.

That question now seemed academic to him. Buddy Wojcik was a good story teller. He had made Mary Waskowski so real that Jim felt as though he had seen her. It was a story that the old man must have repeated thousands of times. Jim was jolted by the memory of the box, that it actually existed and that Janice now had it. He would prefer to cut off thought about that, except to decide how he would report that twist.

Janice was numb. She had set out on a ghost-finding expedition, risking the wrath of Eddie to do it. The experience she had at the mental hospital was as though someone had blown a strange wind through her soul. Every pore of her body had been open to listen and respond as the details came from the elderly man. In all the ghost stories she had read or seen in the movies, people either went crazy or immediately recovered in time for the next scene. She had not. Her speech, her feelings and her sensitivities remained fresh and new to her. She was not even aware of what road they were on. She was experiencing Resurrection Mary, and it was all familiar to her. A door had been broken down and she felt as if she could fly if she had to.

Jim sensed something wrong with the steering of the car, but then it had seemed to adjust itself. He was, he concluded, just imagining it. If you drive a car ten years old, you get used to its quirks. You have to have faith in the vehicle and not panic at every slight aberration.

"Old Betsy, you do need a check-up," he half-whispered, addressing the car.

Janice continued her silence. Jim wished he could have taken a photo of her as she had listened to the story of Resurrection Mary. Her stare had been intense, her mouth slightly open. She had nodded at each word as the old man spoke.

How had he himself really been affected? He was still not certain. Thoughts had to settle. Maybe, after the story was written.

They traveled more than a mile farther on the tree-enshrouded Archer Avenue. The night seemed to grow even darker and they had yet to pass another car.

"I wish I had stayed on the expressway," Jim thought. "We could have been near Janice's house by now."

He was feeling the weariness of the day, the exhaustion that comes at the end of an emotional experience.

Ever so slightly, he pressed down on the accelerator.

It was a rattling noise at first and then, a god-awful

clanking sound. It came from the rear, on his side. Heavy metal was grinding against heavy metal, and all that noise somehow was encased by the sound of something hitting against steel.

Something was wrong, possibly seriously wrong. And he was traveling much too fast to control the problem.

Jim was afraid to hit the brakes or even pump them. Maybe the sound would stop suddenly and go away. Once before, it seemed, something like this had happened. That time, the impending disaster had gone away. Maybe it had been a nightmare or a hundred of them from which he had awakened. But, this was not a dream. The wrenching pull of the wheel and the terrifying noise continued. The clattering sound knifed into a hard, metallic screech that pierced his ears.

Control of the car was grabbed abruptly from his hands, as he witnessed a bizarre, fearsome sight—the rear wheel on the driver's side went speeding past his door and shot off into the woods. There was no longer any possibility of controlling the car or of altering what was going to happen.

೪

CHAPTER THIRTEEN

ↀ

Thursday evening, October 31

Tomorrow, November 1, 1968, would be All Saints Day, a "holy day of obligation," a day on which it would be a mortal sin for Catholics not to attend Mass. It would also be "First Friday." On this particular day of the month the more devout members of the faith would have a chance, by going to Mass and worthily taking Holy Communion, to obtain a plenary indulgence. This spiritual cleansing would clear the soul of all punishment for past transgressions that normally would await one in Purgatory.

The evening before was for preparation, for going to Confession and making oneself "worthy." Seven parishioners committed to this preparation stood in line against the cinder block sides of the parish church. These walls were lined at five-foot intervals with brown wooden plaques depicting the scenes of the Stations of the Cross. Three babushkaed women waited with rosaries in their hands. Heavy draperies poorly protected the young man kneeling in the confessional from being over-heard.

"Name of the Father, Son and Holy Ghost. Forgive me father for I've sinned. I didn't stop somebody's death. Also I lied twice and hit my little sister."

"You what, my son?"

"Which part?" Junior Grady asked, not certain he had not slurred over enumerating his lesser sins.

"About somebody's death."

"It was a car accident."

"The Church considers it a serious matter if you were driving carelessly and somebody died as a result. Were you drinking?"

"No, father. You don't understand. I wasn't anywhere near the car. My friend did it."

"Then the sin is your friend's. Many people want to take responsibility for what others do because they feel guilt. But you can't confess another person's sin no matter how guilty you feel. Do you understand?"

"I do," Junior said. "But you don't. My friend deliberately did somethin' to somebody's car so that they'd have an accident and be killed."

"What is this you're telling me?"

"My friend was angry at his girlfriend and he saba, saba..."

"Sabotaged?"

"Yeah, to her car."

"Was she killed?"

"No. It ain't happened yet."

"You must prevent it, then."

"That's why I'm here. I had a chance and I didn't tell her. They drove to another city, and I can't now."

"My son, this is serious."

"Yeah, I know, Father."

"Why? Why didn't you tell?"

"Well, this other kid. I like him a lot. I mean, he's cool. I mean, you have to know him. I don't want him in trouble."

"You have to go to the police about this."

"No."

"You have to."

"I will not."

"Why?"

"It's one thing to tell God about Eddie, but it's another to tell the cops. I won't do it. I don't want him in trouble."

"Then God won't forgive you."

"He will if you tell him to. The sisters taught me that in school."

"That's not exactly how it is. I can't give you forgiveness.

I doubt you are even sorry."

"I am sorry. I feel real sorry for her."

"That is not enough. Under the circumstances, I cannot grant you absolution."

"Then to hell with it."

"My son, do you realize what you are doing? You are choosing this other boy over God."

"Yeah, but I have to."

Archer Avenue, the same time

The disabled car containing Jim and Janice shot down Archer Avenue, trapping and sealing them with its speed. Their headlights, reflecting back from wild, natural surroundings, added to the horror of the cataclysm into which they were being hurdled.

Jim could hear the axle abrasively slice into the cement. He felt an empty emotion, a sense of incompleteness as his life rushed toward its unprepared-for conclusion. What was the difference? His heart wanted answers to assuage its fright. A goodbye to anyone? His daughter? A story he had not finished. His dirty laundry at home in a pile. This girl he had gotten into this situation. What would his daughter say? Would his ex-wife cry? It was a horrible vortex without a solid reference point. He gripped the wheel as tightly as his hands could endure, but control was not there. What could he do? He felt the muscles in his face tense. His white, almost bloodless hands were beyond the point of pain.

The journalism review article. He should have written it. Something in him laughed sarcastically. The grinding noise got shriller. Jim's frantic mind ignored it. His muscles tightened and jumped. He tried to send them calming messages, but they were panicking. Finally his foot did what his mind repeatedly had urged it not to do it. It slammed down hard on the brakes.

Janice, stunned out of her silence, screamed. She pushed

her hands against the dashboard as his actions brought an even louder screeching sound than the one already filling the car and piercing their eardrums. The car spun and went into a slide, and headed sideways, the passenger side first, screeching down Archer Avenue. Disaster, danger, death flew terrifyingly down the middle of Archer Avenue. Within seconds the car would start tumbling until it veered off and crashed into anything strong enough to stop it. Glass would shatter. Steel would bend and twist. Bodies, their bodies, would be mangled into the terrifying reality of death. The roadway had become totally dark as the headlights reflected off the trees by the side of Archer Avenue.

Every little thing that had ever happened to them would be culminated in the violent fate awaiting the pair thrown together in the front seat of the vehicle. Then, for a second, time stopped, as though something in a bleep of the continuum were readjusting. Only a fraction of a moment. Then another crescendoing, rushing sound came from behind the screech of the crashing vehicle—a noise with a powerfully growing force behind it.

This new sound, that of a forceful and driving wind pushing through a canyon, overtook the careening automobile as a cat would a mouse. Jim, in a stupor, barely noticed. He had entered a state of shock, traumatically preparing his nervous system for the sharp metal and glass about to knife and to cut into his body.

Violently and suddenly the car was bumped on the driver's side and then thumped again, very hard. Whatever had overtaken the crashing vehicle was attacking the car, playing demolition derby with it.

Once more, that force crashed against the vehicle, strangely straightening its course on the road and, and at the same time, slowing it down. It banged again. Jim's heart had stopped or very nearly had done so. Something larger than the car was rushing along parallel to the automobile, forcing its course.

Jim Rooney could not force his eyes to look at what was six inches outside his window, but he was aware that it was huge and was darker than the night. He could not look, and he did not want to do so.

The car, riding on three wheels, had slowed and was veering almost gently off to the side of Archer Avenue, its speed decreasing to a few miles an hour.

The vehicle was bumped one last time, nudging it up against a tree.

The inevitable had been avoided. They were not dead. The car was damaged, but they were alive and unhurt.

Jim sat stunned, in a trance of physical and emotional shock. Moments passed as wisps of smoke disappeared into the air, as if from a fire.

Throughout his life Jim had seen himself as a most logical human being. Sentences he had written had periods. Things he said or thought could be diagrammed. Logic not only moved atoms, but also governed all of the universe and its existence.

What had just happened?

Jim Rooney did not know. What he experienced had not a punctuation mark based in logic. It rather had dangled and was like a whole paragraph without a comma, a period, or capitalization.

Jim tried to open his door to get out of the car. It had been rammed shut.

Janice was staring wordlessly, as though someone were speaking to her. He looked at her, smiled, and gave her a thumbs up sign. Then Jim carefully climbed over her and got out of the wrecked car.

He looked around, not at the crash, but at the dark woods surrounding him. He tried to return to his normal breathing. He walked a little and then bent down and picked up some dirt. Jim had been at this spot before, he remembered. He turned back to the car. A smile of relief played out on his face.

"Janice," he said, "This is it. This is the place where you heard the requiem music."

Jim did not get a response. He looked into the car.

Janice was gone.

CHAPTER FOURTEEN

cs

A bar on Wabash Avenue

Sunday afternoon, November 17

"You know when you called my apartment yesterday, I was looking out the window and watching some geese. They were flying north. Can you believe that, they were flying the wrong way?"

As Jim spoke, he played with his glass, pretending it was a ouija board indicator.

"There is an explanation and I know I have it." Sarah's voice was gentle.

"About the geese?" Jim asked.

"No, about Janice and about what happened."

"I don't know what happened," he answered in a flat voice. "I don't know where she went, how or why. I don't know what happened before she disappeared, either."

"I believe she realized Eddie had tried to kill both of you, that he had caused the wreck." Sarah looked directly at Jim.

"Possibly."

"Well, she was terrified. The poor kid suddenly figured out how evil her Eddie was. She split. I would have run."

"She ran? She not only ran, but she's still missing. It's two and a half weeks later."

"No, she more than ran. Janice escaped."

"You said something like that when you called yesterday. I just don't know."

"I do," Sarah said. "I know with all my heart."

"It makes some sense. She told me in the car that she

would have escaped if she were Resurrection Mary."

"See what I mean."

He looked at Sarah. For a week his eyes had focused in the woods, looking for a figure lying on the ground or some evidence that Janice had been there, had run that way. Now, Jim slowly began to relax, possibly for the first time since the accident and Janice's disappearance.

"I appreciate what you are trying to do," he said. "I really like it that you called. I mean, I don't have anyone else to talk to about Janice and that bizarre accident."

"You know I escaped," she said. "It was from my relationship with Eddie's father. And believe me it was an escape. That's why I know that she did."

"Your cop friend's rotten, truly the appropriate person to have spawned Eddie. I am very glad that you escaped, Sarah. You certainly seem too fine a human being for him. You're a very nice person."

"Thanks. Them's kind words. I know you're really worried about Janice, but I'd be worried even more if I knew she hadn't escaped, whatever way she did it."

"Your explanation make some sense. It's really the only one that does. Still, somehow, it doesn't quite fit the girl I had come to know. To make such a decision and carry it out in an instance! Janice?"

"A lot of strange things happened," Sarah spoke calmly. "You said so yourself. Her world got turned upside down by Eddie. She realized it."

"I spent seven straight days looking for her in the woods along Archer Avenue. So did a bunch of other people. We thought she might have been dazed from the accident. We didn't find a trace, not a trace."

"She's gone," Sarah said. "She's not in those woods. She was scared, but she knew what she was doing."

"I hope she's all right. I certainly hope so, Sarah."

"She is. And she escaped. You should know that."

"You're right, probably. You certainly are right about a lot of strange things happening. That accident keeps being replayed in my mind. I remember it more as a surrealistic dream than as a real experience. It might have happened in some form, but it didn't happen to me. It was a dream, and maybe this is all still part of it."

"I can understand. It must be painful."

"It is, Sarah. It's just awfully strange, and it's, yes, painfully so. I tried to find her boyfriend. He's gone too. That's what scares me. His family could not be more tight-lipped about his whereabouts."

"I don't know. I haven't talked to Ed."

"I'm not asking you to."

"Janice is all right. I wonder if she feels as free as I do."

"I wonder how Janice feels about anything. And, then, there's your uncle. Talk about strange. Still, I liked him."

"Yes, a dear old guy. He has a sweet innocence."

"I feel bad about my encounter with him. After we left, I wanted to go back. He gave us something—a story, a ribbon, his time. I didn't even give him a handshake. You don't meet someone like him every day. I left so abruptly."

"You feel bad about it?"

"Yes, I do."

"I got an idea."

The bartender suggested another round. Jim looked to his companion and got a nod. He motioned "yes" for both of them.

"Want to go see him again?"

Jim picked up his glass and sipped at his drink.

"Yes," he said. "Let's do it."

"Hah!" Sarah chuckled.

"Why are you laughing?"

"The last time I took someone on a trip downstate I had an ulterior motive. I just think it's funny."

"That was with the cop?"

"You bet."

"Great, Sarah. It's a good idea."

"When can you go?"

"How about Friday? I have it off."

"Yes," Sarah said, "Friday."

"Junior's gonna get it," Eddie resolved. "He will regret trying to avoid me. He's gonna regret it big."

Eddie was angry, and in a black mood.

There had been the accident and everything had gone wrong since it, everything. Where the hell was Janice, the little bitch? Where was she? Nobody knew or else they weren't telling.

Somehow the reporter had escaped the accident and had tried several times to leave a message at Eddie's house. Eddie thought of confronting him about what had happened to Janice, where he was hiding her.

Junior had not returned his calls. Imagine, Junior not returning a call from Eddie. Yeah, he was going to get it big, the stupid fool. And he was going to get it now.

Eddie formulated his plan as he drove. He was going to turn Junior in for theft at the factory, grand theft. Yeah, Junior was the one who was always stealing from Eddie's boss, Sarge. Eddie had played with the plan before and planted several items in the attic of Junior's house so he could execute the plan instantly, as he saw fit.

But he was hesitating. Without Junior or Janice around, Eddie was feeling jarred, painfully alone, and frustrated because things he wanted were not getting done. With a little energy and a fistful of distractions, he could make all the blackness go away, at least for a while.

The car was heading to Junior's for a showdown, but also one last chance. Eddie might let his companion off relatively easy if he offered to eat a little dirt.

"Yah, that's it," Eddie said to himself. "I'll make him eat some dirt—literally. Otherwise, pow! I mean he's really gonna get it. Even if he eats the dirt, I still might turn him in. Not return a call, will he?"

Archer Avenue had swung south and he had passed Roberts Road when he saw a girl ahead. She was walking with her back to him. Was it Janice? She had blonde hair. It was not

Janice's hairdo, but if she had let her hair down, it could be. He felt pained with anger. He hoped it was Janice; yes, he really hoped it was. He was traveling too fast to stop or even slow down.

He made a fast U-turn and drove slowly along Resurrection Cemetery, trying to get a better look. She looked like Janice. Still, he couldn't be sure, so he did another U-turn and pulled up along side of her.

Was it Janice or wasn't it?

He stopped next to her, ready to tell her to get in. He fingered the roll of coins he kept in his pocket. This time as he hit her, she would feel it.

She took the handle, pulled the door open, and got into the car.

It was not Janice.

"Get out," he ordered.

She did not obey him. She stared intensely, as if through him. Her face was puffy. She was young. Her eyes—he couldn't look away from them.

"Get out," he commanded.

She slid over on to the seat next to him.

"Get the hell away from me," he said.

She slowly opened his shirt and reached her hand down under his shirt. Her hand, her hand was cold!

A scream, initially a response to the sudden and surprising chilly feeling, erupted from him.

He shut his eyes and tried to well up his most vehement anger to use against her. All he could resurrect, however, was a sound that was part babble and part whine.

She moved closer. She was attempting to kiss him and he was helpless to even move, to raise his arm to push her away, much less to hit her.

Her lips touched his.

Peoria State Mental Hospital

Noon, Friday, November 22

"Was it sudden?" the assistant superintendent asked.

"Yes," the ward nurse said, "he died this morning. He was looking out the window and he just keeled over."

"What was his name, Wojak?"

"Wojcik."

"Was he the oldest inmate?"

"I'm sure he was. The records show he entered the state hospital at Dunning in 1899, 69 years ago."

"You know," the assistant superintendent said, "I've been here 30 years and he has been hospitalized more than twice that long and I never talked to the man. He looked more withdrawn than catatonic or schizophrenic. They wouldn't even put someone like that in a hospital today."

"He was all right here," the nurse said. "A young aide on nights, a girl who just started here last week, really took a shine to him."

"Maybe he couldn't take the attention," the assistant superintendent said.

"Maybe he died happy," the nurse mused.

"What does it matter," the hospital official answered. "We got an open bed now. We can give it to the new intake. The kid with the Polish last name."

"What's wrong with him?"

"Now, that one's really nuts."

"Have you read his file?"

"I glanced at it. He was brought in by his father, a cop. Something about having been seduced by a ghost."

❧

OTHER BOOKS BY CHICAGO HISTORICAL BOOKWORKS

Dillinger: A Short and Violent Life. By Robert Cromie and Joseph Pinkston. (1962) Reprint.
 Classic biography of an extraordinary American folk hero and bankrobber.
 Softcover $10.95

The Cliff Dwellers: The History of a Chicago Cultural Institution. By Henry Regnery.
 This book spans the history of the club from its auspicious beginnings to the present.
 Hardcover $20

If Christ Came to Chicago. By William T. Stead. (1894) Reprint.
 One of the most soul-stirring, muck-raking books ever written about an American city.
 Softcover $14.95

Catalogue of the WPA Writers' Program Publications: September, 1941. By the WPA Writers' Program. (1941) Reprint.
 A catalogue listing more than 1,000 WPA books, plays, pamphlets, etc.
 Softcover $ 7.50

A Bibliography of Illinois, Chicago, and Environs. By the WPA Writers' Program. 1937) Reprint.
 A guide to literature and materials prior to 1937 on the state of Illinois, the city of Chicago, and its suburbs.
 Softcover $15

The Chicagoization of America: 1893-1917. By Kenan Heise.
 Fascinating evidence of Chicago's profound cultural and moral impact on the rest of the United States between the World's Columbian Exposition and World War I.
 Softcover $12.95

Check List of Chicago Ante-Fire Imprints: 1851-1871. By the WPA Writers' Program. 1938) Reprint.
 Bibliography of 1,880 books and pamphlets printed in Chicago in the 20 years before the Chicago Fire.
 Spiral-bound $35

Alphonse: A Play Based on the Words of Al Capone. By Kenan Heise.
 Contemporary newspapers and the transcript of the trial of Al Capone contributed the material from which this play was written.
 Softcover $ 6.95

The Cost of Something for Nothing. By John Peter Altgeld. (1903) Reprint.
 Strong words from the man whom Darrow called "one of the most sincere and devoted friends of humanity this country has ever produced."
 Hardcover, D.J. $ 9.95